Pip of Pengersick –
An Adventurer's Tale

OR

My Part in
Napoleon's Downfall

GW00728030

www.harveyberrickpublishing.co.uk

Pip of Pengersick –
An Adventurer's Tale

OR

My Part in
Napoleon's Downfall

J. A. C. WEST

HARVEY
BERRICK
PUBLISHING

First published in Great Britain in 2010
Harvey Berrick Publishing, 8 The Links, Pengersick Lane, Praa Sands, Cornwall TR20 9RD

A CIP catalogue record of this book is available from the British Library

ISBN-13 978-0-955315039

Printed in Great Britain by Headland Printers
Designed by Alex Szyszkowski
Cover designed by Nicky Stott
Illustrations by Oliver Lake

To my friends – those with two legs and those with four.

PIP OF PENGERSICK

———⟶•⟵———

AN ADVENTURER'S TALE
OR
My Part in Napoleon's Downfall

———⟶•⟵———

The TRUE STORY concerning Adventures on the
High Seas regarding PERSONS OF RENOWN and
PERSONS OF FUR with respect to the Brave and Fearless
MEN OF KERNOW who knew NO FEAR against the might
of the Army of the DASTARDLY WOLF OF FRANCE,

NAPOLEON BONAPARTE.

And also with RESPECT to the most
HIGHLY REGARDED and BEST BELOVED

ADMIRAL HORATIO NELSON

and his STEADFAST COMPANIONS of both
TWO LEGS and FOUR LEGS and the Role herein
played by said NOBLE BEASTS.

*An Interesting and Original True Story from the Writer of "Pip of
Pengersick – A Smuggler's Tale", as Reported to the Author.*

———⟶•⟵———

Dedicated to HIS ROYAL HIGHNESS PRINCE GEORGE.

———⟶•⟵———

*NOTE: Persons of Sensitive Dispositions should proceed
with the UTMOST CAUTION.*

PENZANCE, 13 March, 1806

CHAPTER ONE

Wreckers!

From Wicked Rocks and Shelving Sands,
From Breage and Germoe men's hands,
Dear Lord deliver Us.

Cornish sailors' saying

The wind howled with the first of the Autumn storms and the slates danced across the roof but I was warm and dry and, if the truth be told, fast asleep in front of a merry fire.

Harry snored companionably in his armchair, mouth open and newspaper wrinkled on his lap – a scene of the utmost domestic tranquillity you can be sure.

I cannot tell what first roused me from satisfying dreams of wreaking revenge on the local rabbit population who, with alarming regularity, destroyed the neat ranks of spinach in Harry's vegetable patch.

Now wide awake, I strained to hear above the gale that sent squalls of salt-laden rain thundering against our cottage windows. And then I heard it – the sound once heard that is never forgot – the sound of men screaming – the sound of men drowning.

I barked sharply and Harry awoke with an oath.

"What is it, little maid?" he said, rather gruffly.

I barked again and stood pointedly by the door.

"Surely you do not wish to go out on such a gorming night! It's roaring like Cudden, wadna you!" said Harry.

1

It must be said that Harry is one of my favourite humans but even he could be remarkably slow on the uptake.

To make my point more forceful, I fastened my teeth into his oilskin coat, wrestled it from its hook and dragged it to the door.

Harry's annoyance turned to concern, his kind face furrowed at the brow.

"Have you heard something? Is something wrong?"

I barked again in the affirmative.

Harry reluctantly struggled into his oilskins and fumbled to find his sou'wester as I pawed impatiently at the door.

He took the precaution of bringing an oil lamp to light his path – something of which I have no need, being gifted with the excellent night sight of my kind.

As soon as Harry lifted the latch, the door was wrenched open by the gale and I was forced to jump back sharpish, for fear of being squashed quite flat.

The howling wind drove my ears back as I tore down the lane that led from our small village to the headland.

The path was rough underfoot and I could hear Harry cursing behind me as he stumbled through the mud, tripping on stones.

Quick as we had been, by the time we scrambled to the cliff edge, the moans of the drowning men had quite died away. All we could see was the remains of a splendid galleon pinned to the treacherous rocks of Rinsey Head, the top mast broken, the canvas sails shredded into ribbons.

We stared with a horrid fascination as again and again the galleon was dashed against the unfeeling rocks by the relentless sea.

"God rest your poor souls," whispered Harry.

He turned to look down at me.

"There's nothing we can do for them, little maid. We are too late."

———◆———

Word of the tragedy spread far and wide. The small communities of this part of western Cornwall measured their

lives by the seasons and the benevolence or fury of the sea and many a family knew the grief of losing a son or husband at sea.

By morning scores of men and women from the nearby villages of Germoe, Ashton, Breage and Pengersick, the village where I had been born, stood waiting for low tide, ready to descend the cliffs, to bury any dead that might be found – and to enjoy the privileges of wreckers. The law had it that wreckage was the property of the finders, should it be that no man nor animal were left alive from a shipwreck. This, legend had it, has brought about the untimely deaths of several shipwreck survivors and is something of which that I, as a Cornish maid, am not proud. But the people were poor and wretched and my sympathies were divided. On this occasion there were no survivors found. Besides, the rich pickings of a wrecked galleon could mean the difference between a good year and a hungry one.

The men and women of these local villages had a fearsome reputation and many foreigners from Devon and beyond believed that they even caused shipwrecks by waving lanterns from the cliffs to tempt desperate ships onto the jagged rocks below. This, of course, is nonsense. I have spent much time at sea and it has always been the case that should anyone spy a lantern in the midnight gloom, 'tis a sure sign of land and the ship's captain will urgently order the ship away from such dangerous shores. What man of sense would steer his ship towards a certain death?

As the tide slowly retreated I scampered down the slippery granite path to the beach and wandered through the sad pieces of timber, rope and personal belongings that were strewn across the sand. I was halted in my tracks by the sight of a pale, drowned boy – a child who was not much older than I.

His sightless eyes were open to the sky and I wondered if his mother would ever know what had become of him.

Some Christians believe that beasts such as I are without souls and when we die we will cease to exist with no entry to Heaven and the comfort of Our Lord. I would tell these people, should they ask me, that God knows I have a soul and that I prayed for the young boy that his was Heaven-bound that fateful morning.

Harry joined me on the beach and leaned down to close the child's eyes – a boy who could no longer look upon the world. He muttered a few indistinct words over the poor corpse and made the sign of the cross. A winding sheet was fashioned from a piece of sailcloth and the small body was carried up the cliff in a silence as deep as death.

The hulk of the galleon was flayed on the black rocks, seaweed like mermaid's hair clinging to the shattered carcass. 'Twas a sorry sight indeed, but magnificent in its way: a leviathan doomed to rot in this remote cove.

I had noticed that the young boy's clothes were not as those worn by youngsters in my village. I decided he must be from foreign shores. This was confirmed when by happy accident my foraging led me to stumble upon a crate of the food that I desire most in the world: garlic sausage!

I tore through the side of the wooden crate with great urgency and looked sternly at anyone who came near me. This was my wrecker's find and no-one would take it from me. Harry disapproved of me eating garlic sausage due to some rather unfortunate side effects that later occurred, but perhaps he would be forgiving if this time I shared my bounty with him. Perhaps.

I wrestled the largest of the sausages free from the crate and sank my teeth into a small piece of heaven, closing my eyes in anticipation of the delights to come.

To my surprise, my advance through the delicious treat was interrupted by something that was definitely not supposed to be part of the ingredients – a thick piece of rolled up parchment. What a way to treat a garlic sausage! I was about to tear the offending document into shreds when it occurred to me that someone who had taken such efforts to hide a document in the middle of a garlic sausage must have a secret – maybe an important one.

I decided to take the parchment to Harry.

"What have you found there, my digy maid?" said Harry.

He frowned as he looked over the parchment. "'Tis written in foreign," said Harry. "I don't recognise a single word."

He sniffed at it. "Where on earth did you find this?"

Sometimes 'tis useful to be a person of fur and have no blushes; instead I wagged my tail.

Harry fixed me with a stare then said, "I'll take it to Reverend Grylls over at Breage. Maybe he'll know what to make of it. I don't suppose it's anything important."

On that point I begged to differ: it seemed to me that even the dullest of humans would not take to hiding a document inside a garlic sausage unless it be of the highest import. But as I did not wish to embarrass Harry further, I decided to make no more of it at that time.

Instead I returned to the crate of garlic sausages, ate what I could not carry and buried the rest in a convenient location away from the prying eyes of the other wreckers.

<hr/>

The boy was laid to rest in an unremarked corner at the church of St Breaca in the parish of Breage. It was a short service but many villagers attended. The sight of the drowned boy had moved many a hard heart and each mother felt that this could have been her lad and each father felt that the loss of a son was a terrible thing.

After the service Harry spoke to Reverend Grylls in his well appointed cottage. It was delightful for me because I had the opportunity to visit with my brothers Bryok and Cadan who had moved in with the vicar to take advantage of his wife's gentle nature and the best dinners in the parish.

Harry and I were shown into the drawing room at the Rectory.

Bryok had grown fat and comfortable and yawned and stretched and wagged a languid tail at my arrival. Cadan, still slim and active, bounded from the fire, wagging his whole body, such was his pleasure to see me. He escorted me to the best spot on the rug by the fire and we made ourselves comfortable as the humans went about their business.

I could see that the Reverend Grylls was not happy to be entertaining at a time when he usually took his sherry: whether this were because he did not wish for our company, or whether he did not wish to share his best Spanish sherry with Harry, I could not tell.

"Very well," he said sharply, "and what is it you have to show me, Mr Carter?"

It later occurred to me that the Reverend Grylls did not like to share his drawing room with folk such as Harry and I – that is, persons who did not have their own gig-cart but relied upon legs to transport them from here to there. On the other hand, neither did he wish to affront the persons who provided him with his smuggled Spanish sherry in the first place.

"I came across this document in the wreckage of that unfortunate galleon," said Harry. "'Tis likely nothing, but I wondered if you might be able to tell me something of it."

Only two things delighted the Reverend Grylls, apart from his Spanish sherry: a good dinner and a chance to show off his book learning, which was considerable.

"Aha! Splendid! Splendid! Now let me see. Well, I can tell you it is not French, nor is it Latin. I do believe it is Spanish. How interesting. Did that galleon have the look of a Spaniard about it? I'll probably find this is no more than a shipping manifesto, but I will look into it for you, Mr Carter, you can be sure."

That evening as Harry and I returned from an evening stroll under the bright Autumn stars, we heard the distinctive sound of Reverend Grylls' gig-cart rattling down our lane. Something very particular must have drawn him from his comfortable Rectory at this hour. Indeed he looked paler and more troubled than I could ever recall seeing him.

"Oh, Mr Carter. Thank goodness you are at home, Sir. This is most distressing. Most distressing indeed!"

Harry bade him sit down and gave him a glass of rum, which Harry swore by for people who had had a shock, (or an ailment, or good news, or, in fact, on just about any occasion you could name).

I saw that the Reverend's hands were shaking ever so slightly. The poor fellow really looked worried and was wisnt indeed.

"This document," he said, speaking in an urgent tone, "I have translated. It is, as I surmised, in Spanish. It tells, oh dear, I can hardly say it... it tells of a plan, an agreement between France and Spain to band together as allies; to become an enemy of the Crown of England. This, I suppose is no surprise since that upstart Napoleon Bonaparte crowned himself Emperor last Christmas."

He paused, and I could see he was steadying his nerve to tell something of great moment.

"This document describes a plan to attack the Third Coalition – that is to say – to attack Britain. A vast army of 180,000 troops is being amassed near to Boulogne as I speak, at this very second!"

Harry looked serious.

"My good man, it gets worse," said Reverend Grylls. "The plan states that the invasion will begin here – in Cornwall!"

CHAPTER TWO

Speaking in tongues

Del dicho al hecho hay un buen trecho.
(Between saying and doing there is a great gap.)

Spanish proverb

Harry seemed turned to stone. I sensed he was deeply shocked and I licked his hand to give him what comfort I could.

The Reverend Grylls, on the other hand, had become most animated, his face an alarming beetroot colour.

"My dear sir! Do you not see? Can you not tell? This is information of the direst description! It must be taken forthwith to those who can act upon it. It must be taken to London at once."

Harry stared into the fire.

His stillness spurred on the Reverend Grylls to a state of near apoplexy.

"My good man! We must not waste a single moment!"

Harry raised his eyes. "I have been to London. I did not like it."

The Reverend spluttered incoherently.

"I do not think London is the place for this message to be taken," said Harry, at length. "The King is ill – they say he has lost his wits – and I do not know who there would take my message. I have no way of reaching the Prince – or of being believed by men who would or could take action. My hope – and that of all the country – rests with another."

"Who on earth are you talking about?" said the Reverend in a moderately calmer manner.

"I shall take this document to Admiral Horatio Lord Nelson," said Harry softly. "He has left London and is now quartered at Portsmouth awaiting his moment to strike. He will know what to do. He will know how to act."

The Reverend was silent and I looked up expectantly: who indeed had not heard of Lord Nelson, the conqueror of Copenhagen, the hero of the Battle of the Nile? Nelson was the man who had taken on the Wolf of France and sent him packing once before. Napoleon's army had been stranded in Egypt when Lord Nelson addressed himself to the French. Napoleon himself fled back to France, abandoning his men to their fate. If that is the work of a Republican, then give me a King any day!

I felt excited about meeting Lord Nelson, this giant amongst men, and wondered how tall he really was. For I was and am just a little thing, though my heart is big.

"Yes, indeed!" said Reverend Grylls. "That is a most felicitous plan. I would urge you to attempt this with all expedition!"

"That I shall," said Harry, thoughtfully. The Reverend seemed positively exuberant now that Harry had taken the weight of responsibility from him.

"One thing more," said Harry. "No-one must know of this. Have you told anyone of what you have learned?"

"My dear man," said the Reverend looking peeved. "I am not in the habit of tittle-tattling with women and servants. I have communicated this information to you and you alone."

"Good," said Harry. "Then let us keep it that way. This information could prove most dangerous to the man who knows it. The Spanish, or indeed the Frenchies, will be happy to kill that man, for we are at war."

The Reverend looked pale again and was unusually quiet as he swallowed quickly several times.

"Yes, yes indeed. I see your point – debated most succinctly. I shall speak not a word to any man."

"And when the foreigners come looking for their lost ship, which they surely shall, 'twill be best if they do not find you and that you make yourself scarce. Perhaps there is some cousin in a distant place that you can visit until this is over?"

Now the Reverend was not what I would call a man of action. In fact the most active he had ever been was in loudly declaiming the ferocity of his God from the pulpit and, most recently, in communicating the extraordinary information he had just passed to Harry; but he puffed out his chest and lifted his chin.

"No, indeed! God has chosen me to be the shepherd of my flock. I will not abandon them in their hour of need. If and when the Spanish – or French – do come, we will face them together and, with God's blessing, shall not be the worse for our encounter."

Harry smiled briefly and shook the Reverend's hand. "Then I shall say farewell to you, sir. We will be off in the morning."

"'We'?" said the Reverend, frowning.

Harry pointed at me and I wagged my tail. "'We'," he said.

The Reverend jogged back up the darkened lane in his trap, collar turned to the westerly wind that blew steadily from the sea.

Harry discussed his plans aloud. "Though it would be faster to sail to Portsmouth," he said, "I dare not take the chance that a Spaniard or French ship will find us. They'll be looking, sure enough, scramming around for us. We could not outrun a warship. No, we must go overland. A man and his dog will not cause much comment."

I bared my teeth. I would make the upstart Bonaparte rue the day when he declared war on Cornwall!

———⇒•⇐———

We left our home before dawn not knowing how many weeks, or indeed months, it would be before we crossed the familiar threshold once more.

Harry slipped and slithered on the muddy track; my keener eyes allowed me to trot along quite contentedly. None of our neighbours were about, 'though twice I smelt the smoke from a chimney and once caught the delicious scent of fried baggly-ow, a sort of dried codfish cooked with cabbage.

My stomach rumbled and I looked hopefully at Harry but he strode on. I sighed. Breakfast, it seemed, was of a lesser importance than our mission. I wondered, not for the first time, if Harry's priorities were quite the same as mine.

We walked briskly and soon passed the lane that led down to the village of my birth. I say 'village' for a small community had grown up at Pengersick, but 'twas better known for the crumbling castle that glowered down on the tumble of granite cottages. I often wandered down there to spend a quiet hour among the forlorn ghosts.

But today we had urgent business and no time for reminiscing. I trotted next to Harry as we marched along the Penzance road at a smart pace towards the house of Harry's brother.

I was glad of this because it meant that I could pass the time of day with my old friend and comrade, Jethro, whose equine lineage stretched back to the famous Godolphin Arabian racehorse, with a fair few twists and turns along the way, it must be said.

Jethro whinnied happily at my arrival. I was shocked to see how old my dear friend had become. He stood uncomfortably on three legs and I could tell his hooves hurt him. His fourth leg was bound up with brown paper and vinegar to help soothe the arthritis that had slowed him down. He was also troubled with a large number of rats who lived in his hay loft and often stole his dinner. I spent an enjoyable hour chasing them from the barn and ensuring that many would not be coming back to bother him again. I hoped Harry would bring me some of his breakfast: fried bacon is always preferable in my opinion – my stomach revolted at the thought of eating fresh rat, though I have heard that those who are starving would not turn down the opportunity.

Harry appeared with his brother John. The family business of smuggling must have been prospering because his belly overhung his stout leather belt by a number of degrees.

"Well, brother," said John, "this is a caudling mess and no mistake. I'll tell any who asks that you've gone to Exeter on business for me. That will keep the coozing and gossipers quiet for a couple of weeks: by then and with a fair wind behind you, you'll be well on with your journey and out of danger's reach."

He loaned us his new saddle horse, Cubert by name: a young, gangly, coltish fellow, without Jethro's comfortable and commodious rear. But he was eager for the adventure and so Harry said his goodbyes and we trotted off along the Penzance road as night shyly became dawn, then turned north and east into the thin morning sun that lighted our way.

The road soon became busy with farm workers on their way

to the fields and miners returning from the night shift underground, their weary tread matching their grey, lined faces. I shuddered at the thought of earning a living so far beneath the earth with the weight of all the world pressing down on me. Some brave souls mined the veins of tin that ran under the bedrock of the sea: in the mine's upper levels you could hear the waves crashing down on the thin layer of granite that supported an ocean above your head. I much preferred Harry's method of earning his living sailing on the sea, not choking in a dark hole beneath it.

We passed a long line of mules loaded with tin and copper ore, the poor beasts each carrying some 300 pounds apiece – the weight of two men. Cubert seemed to hang his head in sympathy and I thanked my stars that I had been born a lucky dog and not a pack animal.

The early coach to Truro bustled past us, laden with baskets and the well-to-do of Penzance in their plain worsted dress and best linen.

Harry waved a jaunty hand at the coach driver and I barked a greeting: part of our plan was to be as noticeable as possible in this early stage of our journey before disappearing into the bustling hoards of the city at Exeter. We hoped that this would lead any who spied on us to believe that we had from thence boarded a ship, which, of course, was not our intention at all.

We planned to night in some comfort at Truro at a rather grand hotel. But the mistress of said hotel sneered down her pointed nose at me, insisting that I be put in the stables for the night. Normally Harry is of a calm and pliable disposition but I am happy to say that he did not take kindly to her suggestion; nor she to his that he would take his business to some friendlier establishment.

In the end the jingle of Harry's purse convinced our hostess that we were patrons worth being pleasant to. I do not like people who have to be paid to be pleasant: I raised my lip at her and Harry blinked in surprise and then tried to hide a smile.

We dined well on rabbit stew, cabbage and potatoes. I was sure the gravy would add an extra shine to my coat as I licked the last drops from my lips. The mistress of the establishment sorely failed to hide her displeasure that a four-legged creature such as I should be eating her fine vittles from her best china. But at least by licking my dish so thoroughly I had saved her some washing up.

We were about to turn in for the night when I heard a commotion in the courtyard below. Harry was immediately on his guard. He blew out the lamp in our room and peered cautiously out of the window. A group of six men and horses milled around the small courtyard: although none were in uniform, it was clear from their military bearing that they were soldiers… and it was clear from their heavily-accented English that they were foreign. But from where? Many travellers landed at Cornish ports and continued their journeys overland on horseback or by coach. But this seemed too much of a coincidence coming after the recent beaching of a Spanish galleon.

"We require rooms and stabling for the night," said the leader. "Do you have room? Do you have many guests?"

"Oh, sir!" fluttered our lady host. "Only one guest tonight and he is no gentleman like you. He let his dog in my dining room. Imagine!"

"It must be hard for a lady of refinement to mingle with the public," said the leader, using more charm than I thought strictly necessary.

"Oh, yes, indeed," the landlady simpered. "Such rough people one meets. So many foreigners… oh… I don't mean you, sir, not at all… indeed not of your quality, of course, sir!"

"No, that is not likely," said the leader with a lift of his chin. "I am Dom Álvaro Vaz de Almada, Count of Avranches, a gentleman trader from Portugal."

His emphasis on that last word did not fool us. Although Portugal was an ally to Britain against the combined forces of Spain and France, a few Portuguese supported Napoleon but as I did not speak Portuguee, who was to say that this new arrival was not really a Spanish spy?

Harry's thoughts were clearly galloping along the same course as mine.

"I don't think we'll risk staying till morning, little maid," said Harry to me. "As soon as they are asleep, we will take our leave."

We waited in silence until the hotel was still. Harry left a few coins on the dresser to pay for our meal and we crept down the stairs and out into the courtyard. A problem presented itself to us immediately: the foreigners had put a guard into the stable block. The glitter of his eyes in the lamplight showed that he took his duty seriously. I should not have been surprised for well I knew that a guard on duty in enemy territory can be shot for falling asleep.

"'Twill not be aisy," murmured Harry to himself, "but perhaps a small distraction will answer?"

I realised immediately that a small black-and-white dog would make a very good distraction to a cold and lonely soldier, far from the comforts and companions of home.

I trotted over to the soldier and sat down beside him. He looked surprised but decided I posed no threat because he proceeded to stroke my head and croon gently in a foreign tongue. I felt almost guilty to deceive him so, but steeled myself as I remembered that business came before pleasure.

Harry's cudgel sounded woodenly as he clubbed the poor soldier senseless. I hoped he would not be in too much trouble for this neglect of his duty, or his head too sore.

Our next problem was how to make good our escape. Cubert's hooves would echo roundly in the cobbled yard and give away our stealthy exit.

Harry's solution was to shred a piece of old blanket and wrap it around each of Cubert's hooves. You will agree that this was a good idea but I was dismayed to see that the blanket used was mine own, and a particular favourite.

"Sorry, little maid," said Harry, as he saw the look upon my face, "but needs must."

I noticed that he didn't shred his own blanket, so decided he should not complain should I wish to snuggle under his in the near future.

The courtyard's gate was locked and barred. Luckily our hostess had left a key in the gate in case guests wished to be early on the road before the household arose, as many did in these rural parts. I held my breath and kept alert as the heavy oak door swung open, squealing only slightly on its old hinges.

We crept out of Truro and continued our journey north and east, keeping a careful eye on our back trail for those who might follow: French, Spanish or Portugee. Our plan to be noticeable had been abandoned. Harry was cautious, shunning major roads and sleeping in empty barns or under the brilliant stars. More than once I saw frost on our blanket when I poked my head out at daybreak. Despite the mildness of these early Autumn days, the nights were chill.

We carefully avoided the great city of Exeter and continued

our journey along the coast road, passing through the pretty Devonshire village of Ottery St Mary, famous for being the birthplace of the celebrated poet, Mr Coleridge. The village inn looked cheerful in the twilight and Harry looked at it wistfully.

"I daresn't go in, little maid," he said, "'though fellowship with another human would be well met for me."

I was rather hurt by his speech. Although I am not the most loquacious of beasts I do feel that I am a good travelling companion, never complaining about the vagaries of human behaviour and always on the alert for villainy from strangers.

Harry must have seen my sad expression because he stroked my fur and pulled my ears gently, saying, "But you are a good friend and I trust you with my life, so we shall continue with our journey, just the three of us, as merry as we can be and as cosy as two bugs in a rug."

Personally I do not like to share my rug with bugs, but humans are peculiar creatures, I find.

>>◦<<

Three more days of hard travel and we reached our journey's end – or so I believed. The naval town of Portsmouth was spread before us, the sea sparkling and the masts of a hundred ships bobbed in the harbour mouth. It reminded me strongly of Falmouth and of home.

Harry's face relaxed into a grin, relieved to have reached safety and far from the reach of the enemy spies who had been following us.

"Now all we have to do is reach my Lord Nelson," said Harry. Some things are easier said than done.

CHAPTER THREE

Portsmouth

Her cwom Port on Bretene his .ii. suna Bieda Mægla mid .ii.
scipum on þære stowe þe is gecueden Portesmuþa ofslogon
anne giongne brettiscmonnan, swiþe æþelne monnan.
(Here Port and his two sons Bieda and Mægla came to
Britain with two ships to the place which is called Portsmouth
and slew a young British man, a very noble man.)

The Anglo Saxon Chronicle, 501AD

Portsmouth was a great town in those days, thronged with naval men longing for the chance to put to sea and show the Wolf of France that England was not to be trifled with. Although not as grand as London, the people of Portsmouth aped its style with many a fine building and gilded carriage splashing through the muddy streets and rattling along newly laid cobbles.

Every second building seemed to cater to the navy in some design or purpose. There were the ropewalks, long wooden buildings where the master spinners toiled to provide the 100 fathoms of rigging required for each of the great ships that flocked to the harbour; there were drinking dens that eased the minds of the sailors soon to put to sea; and everywhere provisions were being taken by cart from the redbrick warehouses through the teeming streets to supply the floating castles of England's fleet.

Harry was happy to be amongst fellow seafarers again. To travel cross-country for a man such as Harry was like putting a racehorse to a plough – it just ought not to be. But here amongst his own seafaring kind, no matter how odd and grating their accents, he was at ease.

I, on the other hand, could not be happy in such a crowded place where every second I had to watch that I wasn't stepped on, squashed, or kicked into the overflowing, stinking gutter. I longed to be home, stretched out before Harry's fireside, with a full belly, the sound of the sea on the shore, and a peaceful mind. Instead I had to practise forbearance and patience – neither of which, I admit, came naturally to me.

Harry secured us lodgings above a small tavern that seemed a little cleaner than the rest (although the fellow travellers that bit me mercilessly and had me scratching from noon till night rapidly disabused me of that idea).

Examining the room closely, Harry found a convenient gap under the floorboards. Carefully he wrapped the Spanish document and Reverend Grylls' translation in a thick oilskin that would keep all secure from damp and rats until both parchments could be safely delivered to my Lord Nelson.

Cubert was comfortably stabled at the rear of the establishment, at great expense, I should add. Saddle horses were something of a rarity and a luxury in this seafaring town. He seemed remarkably content amongst the foreign horses of Portsmouth and munched happily on a net of hay with a few oats mixed in. I rather resented his ease when I was so restless myself.

"Don't be tiffed, little maid," said Harry reassuringly and with unwonted confidence. "We'll not be here long, just a touch-pipe o' time. We'll find my Lord Nelson and deliver this dread document then soon be on our way. Although I confess Portsmouth is a most bosh-boshy, showy place, I wouldn't mind a gander around it. Perhaps we'n should find ourselves a balling green and make like Sir Walter Raleigh with the Spanish Armada knocking at the door."

He laughed at his little joke.

I sighed. Poor Harry. I hated to disabuse him but I really think he meant Sir Francis Drake who played bowls at Plymouth Hoe whilst the Spanish Armada massed before him. Harry's formal education had been sadly neglected.

We wandered the streets, gawping at the many sights afforded by Portsmouth's natural exuberance and a gaggle of unwashed humans. Their noise and babble competed with the gulls who shrieked above our heads. Harry was enthralled; I longed for home.

Suddenly a man came running through the crowd and roughly pushed Harry aside.

"Mark 'ee!" yelled Harry. "What's all the bobberv?"

"It's the Press!" shouted the man as he thundered past. "Run for your life!"

Harry wasted not a moment. The last thing he wanted was to be caught by the press gangs.

Believe it or not, in those days any healthy man could be pressed into service of the King's Navy whether he wanted to or no. It didn't matter if the man had a job or a family or somewhere else he wished to be; the legal kidnapping – or pressing – of men was a scourge upon seafaring communities such as these. And now the Navy's need was very great and very greedy as it sought to take on the might of Napoleon.

Needless to say we showed the press gang a clean pair of heels and tore through the cobbled streets with the speed of a startled jack-rabbit. Other men and boys ran alongside of us, darting rapidly into the intricate maze of alleys that made up the close quarters of the old town.

Harry wheezed to a halt down a muddy side street. "We got the bettermost of 'em," he said. "But perhaps it would be best to deliver the documents and be on our way."

I heartily agreed.

But first we had to find the whereabouts of my Lord Nelson. I looked around as if I would immediately espy a palace fit for an admiral. But all around me were poor, broken houses and down-on-their-luck shops.

Harry slouched into a local ale house. He was right, of course. 'Twas always the best place to find out the latest news and gossip, helped by the loosening of tongues that beer and rum seemed to encourage in humans.

"This kiddlewing is the place for us," he said. "We'll soon learn of the address we want."

Harry was right and yet he was wrong, too.

"Ah!" said the salty gentleman with whom we shortly took up conversation. "You're looking for One-eyed Horace."

Harry looked blank at this surprising statement.

"Our Admiral," he went on. "Lord Nelson."

"Yes, indeed," said Harry, looking relieved at having finally come to an understanding with the old seadog's curious way of talking.

"Well, I can tell 'ee where he's been an' I can tell 'ee where he's going, but I cannot tell 'ee where he is," said the man with an infuriating air.

I would have liked to have bitten him somewhere discomforting to spur him into more distinct expression but Harry was more patient with the old man.

"That's a curious turn of phrase you have, sir," said Harry.

"Aaargh!" said the man, by way of agreement.

There was a short pause while the old man sucked more beer through his toothless mouth.

The old man's pint pot was made of pewter but its glass bottom showed the beer glugging down the black funnel of his throat, a sight that made my stomach lurch unpleasantly. In most towns that had good roads the ale houses supplied tankards with glass bases. This was to ensure that a sober man could see if someone was approaching him whilst drinking, or tell when a shilling had been dropped into his beer by an army sergeant or navy recruiter. For the unlucky man who drank from a tankard with a shilling at the bottom was deemed to have taken the King's Shilling – prest-money – and thus been lawfully recruited to fight for his country: hence the practice of supplying drinking vessels with clear glass bases. A somewhat gentler form of impressment, I suppose, than clubbing a man in the street and dragging him on board a ship. The end result, however, was the same.

"My Lord Nelson was here," said the old man at last, "and sure as eggs are eggs he'll be back again, but I do believe 'ee 'as missed him for he has gone to London by coach, no doubt to take his orders from Admiralty House. And, I hope and believe, to push that damned Bonaparte all the way back to Corsica."

Harry grimaced with frustration.

Our wanderings through Portsmouth meant that we had missed my Lord Nelson by a scant few hours and now he was on his way to London and out of our reach. We had two choices: to follow him as fast as we could, although my Lord travelled by coach; or we could wait here for his return, which surely could not be long with the Corsican wolf baying for English blood just a few short miles away across the English Channel.

Harry looked at me and sighed.

"We wait," he said.

———◦———

Portsmouth had one redeeming feature in my eyes – it was nearly an island, being a short peninsula surrounded by sea on three sides. Unlike the village of my home, there were no proper, sandy beaches, but at least I could smell the salt water and enjoy chasing any impertinent seagull who sought to rest anywhere near me. It wasn't home, but it would do for now.

I was, however, impressed by the safe anchorage afforded by the natural harbours of this part of the coast and the small island of Wight that broke the heavy Channel seas. No fear of wreckers here, I thought.

I spent two days wandering the quays and watching the warships of the fleet being repaired, restocked and revitalised for war. If the odd rat came my way, I gave it a nip and a shake, earning the approbations of many grateful sailors. I was even offered permanent work aboard and, tempted as I was to partake of the glory of being part of Nelson's fine fleet, my path and loyalty lay, as ever, with Harry.

Whilst I spent my time thus, Harry was making himself acquainted with the whys, wherefores and whereabouts of the local smuggling fraternity with a view, I suspected, of enlarging the family business once we were safely delivered of my Lord Nelson's documents.

They were a surly, shifty lot to be sure. All bemoaned the damage to business caused by the reopened war. Generally the Royal Navy, like Nelson, turned a blind eye to the smugglers, but at times like this, their presence was barely tolerated. Many had decamped to Dover, further east along the coast. Portsmouth was bad for business, they said.

On the third evening after my Lord Nelson's hasty journey to London we heard the news that he would shortly be returning by chaise. It was always a source of astonishment to me how quickly news from London could be gossiped over in the ale houses of Portsmouth.

We informed our fearsome landlady that we were for the off and would return shortly to settle with her and collect our belongings. Harry's plan was to tell Lord Nelson of the Spanish papers then fetch him to them rather than risk carrying such precious documents through the busy streets where too many eyes watched and waited.

Our landlady merely glowered at us, being of the belief, it seemed, that promised payment was no payment at all. She folded her arms across her ample bosom and said she would look forward to the moment of feeling the weight of Harry's money.

Harry was a little disconcerted and smiled uncertainly, backing from the room, as we heard the rattle of horses' hooves in the thoroughfare outside.

My Lord Nelson must have travelled through the night because his chaise and tired horses arrived in the thin light of dawn.

Looking pale and tired and much smaller than I had expected, Lord Nelson dismounted, stopped briefly at his fine lodgings and walked the short distance through the cheering Portsmouth crowds to his waiting barge. I saw with surprise and sympathy that his right eye was blind and the right sleeve of his blue jacket was quite empty, pinned across the buttons of his narrow chest. My Lord had already given much to his country and yet still he was asked for more. Pity welled up in my heart at the sight.

But such was the popular appeal of my Lord that still more crowds of men, women and children rushed from their homes and swelled the audience along the London road, cheering themselves hoarse in the grey light.

The love and esteem in which they held him was unparalleled, I believe. The crowd pressed towards him eager to touch the hem of his coat or shake the hand of glory; some were kneeling, many praying.

Harry scooped me up to ensure I would not be trodden upon and tried to force his way through the heaving mass.

"My Lord!" he called, his voice lost in the din. "My Lord!"

Harry soon realised that Nelson would not hear him above the huzzahs of the crowd.

"This will never do, little maid," he said. "This bolling crowd will never let us through."

Harry was right. The fetid press of people accompanied the Admiral as he completed his brief journey down to the little beach at Southsea and, with a brief bow to his followers and gracious wave of his hat Nelson boarded the barge that would take him to his vessel, called Victory.

Lining the deck of the enormous battleship stood the marines, resplendent in their red and white uniforms, and the sailors ready to pipe the Admiral aboard.

Harry watched in frustration as eight seamen dressed smartly in white trousers and striped shirts pulled on the oars of the small boat that took Nelson further and further away from us. And away from the vital information that we had to give him.

"Of all the ill luck!" cursed Harry.

"Oh, not at all," said a cold, amused voice. "I think my luck very good indeed."

The icy voice chilled my heart and a low growl began deep in my throat.

Ill luck indeed! Of all the old enemies that we might have run in to, why did it have to be the swaggering bully who stood before us now: the man who had kicked me as a puppy, imprisoned Harry and promised to hang us both?

"Captain Dollard!" said Harry in a strangled voice.

"I am Major Dollard now," came the haughty reply. "You, on the other hand, are still a smuggler: one whom I intend to put out of business – permanently."

He glowed with his triumph over Harry.

A second man stepped into view.

"Major! You have found the man who cheated me. He stole money and several important documents from me."

"It's a lie!" shouted Harry. "You can't trust this man. He says he's Portuguese but he's really a Spaniard!"

"Ridiculous! Will you stop at nothing? Is no insult too great for you?" bellowed Dollard, his face a dangerous purple. "This gentleman," (he stressed the word deliberately, implying that Harry was none such), "this gentleman is Dom Álvaro Vaz de Almada, Count of Avranches, and an ally of this country."

Dollard stumbled slightly over the long, foreign name.

He glared triumphantly at Harry. "Take him away."

The Major's men clapped Harry in irons and dragged him off. One burly soldier grabbed me by the scruff of the neck as I tried to take a chunk out of Dollard's plump behind and I dangled from the man's fist, kicking and yelping. There was nothing Harry could say. There was nothing I could do.

"Revenge, I believe, is a dish best served cold," smiled the man who called himself Dom Álvaro, smiling with satisfaction.

CHAPTER FOUR

An old enemy

The prisoners employed have a pint of beer a day, in addition to the gaol allowance, and are so desirous of being employed in the open air, rather than within the walls of the prison, that a threat of not being allowed to work on the green is found sufficient to keep them in good order.

A description of Launceston prison,
'The West Briton', 14 July 1820

I do not ask, gentle reader, whether you have ever seen the inside of an English prison for I do not wish to offend but, oh! if you had seen what I saw that day, the cries of abhorrence would surely reach the shores of the Orient itself.

Our prison was newly built, being but 10 years old and a far cry from the castle gaol of Launceston with its motte and bailey and ancient, mossy walls.

This prison was built of red bricks and, if the smell of decay was anything to go by, built on damp ground.

The massy brick vaults appeared to have been built on two tiers with the upper level as a vast underground storehouse – the lower level as a stinking gaol.

Harry's body stiffened at the prospect of being dragged inside such a drear place and I cowered in dread beside him.

"We'll hang him in the morning," said Dollard casually, "and the cur."

The man posing as Dom Álvaro frowned. "You will, of

31

course, search him to ensure the return of my belongings first."

Dollard looked irritated.

"Everything will be done that is proper," snorted Dollard, "and then he will be hanged."

"Aye," said Harry, "everything that is proper except a proper trial!"

"Silence!" roared Dollard. All the same, he glanced furtively at his incurious men. "Your trial will be this afternoon. You will be found guilty and hanged from the neck until dead. Proper English justice."

"You can't do this," said Harry in a low voice. "I have my Letter of Marque – from the King himself. It is the King's Will that I go about my trade."

"Then produce this famous Letter," said Dollard in a disbelieving voice.

"I don't carry it with me," said Harry, "but I can send for it."

"All evidence must be produced at your trial this afternoon."

"It'll take days to get here," shouted Harry in sheer frustration.

"Merely a delaying tactic," said Dollard with a bored air, "I know very well that you are a smuggler and that this extraordinary Letter of Marque is a mere fiction and very convenient for you that it is not to hand."

"Not very convenient at all," said Harry, "seeing as you're planning to hang me for the lack of it."

Dom Álvaro was growing more and more impatient.

"Will you please search this criminal so I can be about my own business," he said imperiously.

"Oh very well!" said Dollard with a scowl.

Rough hands searched every pocket, hem and seam of Harry's clothes and even inspected my poor neckerchief, but other than a few pennies, nothing was found.

"I'm afraid your belongings have already been sold on," said Dollard brusquely. "There's nothing here for you. I thank you for your information pertaining to the whereabouts of this villain – you have served the justice of this country well; now I bid you good day."

"But he must have them hidden somewhere!" cried Dom Álvaro. "I must have my belongings returned. You must search his lodgings!"

"Really! I don't have time to go running all over Portsmouth to search every flea-ridden hovel for items that will already have been sold on," snarled Dollard. And with that he turned on his heel and stalked off.

I could see that Dom Álvaro was torn with the desire to have his wishes obeyed and the impossibility of telling Major Dollard the real reason he wanted his 'belongings' – the invasion plans – returned.

Harry and I were dragged away protesting and Dom Álvaro was left fuming in silence.

———⊶•⊷———

The prison gaol was crammed full with men, women and a few ragged children, in varying stages of decay and hopelessness.

The odours that reached my sensitive nose were truly appalling; Harry gagged at the stench, then retched.

I heard the piteous cries of the prisoners, and saw their thin, white arms waving in desperation from the barred windows. We were pushed down the slimy stone steps and thrown into the crowded pit.

Harry was chained by his leg to a small alcove whose wall

shone with filth in the flickering light of the gaoler's oil lamp. He could only sit or crouch, not being given enough room to stand. I was tied up next to him, but some remnant of kindness in the gaoler left me with a long enough rope to be able to reach Harry.

Blank eyes seemed to stare at us from the darkness and I could hear the dull murmuring of those who inhabited this pit of despair. I could not understand why humans treated their fellow creatures with such cruelty.

The noisome odours were almost overpowering and I crept into Harry's arms. I think it comforted him to have me with him in this desolate place.

"Never fear, little maid," said Harry, his voice, cracked with grief and shame, "we've survived worse than this."

I wished rather than believed that Harry was right.

I was also hungry and thirsty and knew that Harry was in the same sorry state. The only moisture dripped from the enslimed walls; yet I couldn't yet bring myself to lick the walls, even to end my raging thirst, but I felt sure the time could not be far off. A rusty pail filled with dank water had been placed in the middle of the cell but none of the other prisoners offered to put it within our reach and Harry did not ask, lost in the gloom of his own thoughts.

As my eyes accustomed to the dark, I could see some of the other prisoners. Whatever condition they had arrived in, they had in time descended so far as they might be called the dregs of humanity. In fact they seemed barely human and you could not call them wild beasts for wild beasts have more dignity than did those sorry creatures.

Their clothes were grey and matted with dirt, torn and barely covering their gaunt bodies. There were old men, young women, small children and newborn babies who had already learned not to cry because crying brought neither relief nor nourishment.

Whatever their age or former position in society they all shared the same haunted, starving expression and I really believed that had not Harry, my guardian, been of such a height and width and strength, I would have been torn limb from limb and eaten on the spot. I trembled at the thought.

The cold and despair were beginning to seep through my fur and into my bones when Harry and I were summarily dragged from our prison pit and hauled before one Dr Sidding, citizen of Portsmouth and Justice of the Peace.

We must have looked and smelled like the foulest of criminals.

Dr Sidding was a tall, thin, cadaverous man with red cheeks and a sour, irritated expression. Small spectacles perched painfully on his angular nose.

"Really Major Dollard, this is most irregular. If, as you say, this man is a career criminal, then he ought to be tried at the Petty Sessions of the Assizes, not here."

"I, we, that is to say, it ought not to be so long in this man's case," blustered Major Dollard. "He is notorious and has escaped from my justice once before. He must be dealt with swiftly."

"Very well, very well," said Dr Sidding. "What are the charges?"

"That he did flee from lawful justice, the sentence of which is hanging from the neck until dead," said Dollard promptly.

"I decide the sentence," said Dr Sidding, giving Dollard a sharp look.

A small flower of hope burst in my chest: perhaps this man

would ensure that Harry and I were treated fairly after all.

"Witnesses?" said Dr Sidding, glowering.

"Yes, sir!" said Dollard triumphantly. "I am a witness. I do declare that on the 13th day of March in the year 1798, as a duly appointed officer of the Customs and Excise, I did

apprehend Harry Carter of Cornwall on the Isle of Bryher with 16 hogsheads of smuggled rum. He was arrested and sentenced but escaped with the help of a number of local criminals. He has been a fugitive from justice ever since."

"I have a Letter of Marque from the King of England!" bellowed Harry. "I am a trader not a smuggler!" A statement which stretched the truth just a little, but needs must, I suppose.

"Rubbish!" said Major Dollard. "A convenient fiction. The man is clearly deranged – and a criminal to boot."

"Hmm," said Dr Sidding again. Then he peered down at me, his expression unreadable.

"And with what is the dog charged? Aiding and abetting, no doubt? A hardened career criminal? Another fugitive from justice?"

Major Dollard's face flushed a dull red. Harry had to hide a grin and I tried to look even smaller and more cowed. Which wasn't hard in the present circumstances, having only recently survived being eaten.

"The beast bit me, sir, and tried to do so again today. "It is a danger to any person who comes near it. It should be drowned."

"Hmm," said Dr Sidding. "I don't suppose there are any witnesses for the defence?"

"No, none," said Major Dollard with quick confidence.

"Yes, sir, there is," came the reply.

My ears pricked up – I knew that voice!

CHAPTER FIVE

An old friend

A good sword and a trusty hand!
A merry heart and true!

'Trelawny', R S Hawker

I stared at the newcomer and cautiously sniffed his trouser leg: it was definitely a scent I recognised from my youth! A sudden torrent of memories flooded through me.

I could see Harry was having more trouble identifying the man if his frown and puzzled air were anything to go by.

"And you are?" said Dr Sidding addressing a short, weatherworn man of indeterminate age.

"Able Seaman Walter Abbot from Honiton, sir, of the Lord Admiral's ship Victory."

Walter Abbot! That was a name from the past indeed! Harry and I had first met Walter in chains, a captive of the slave markets of Salé on the Barbary Coast of Africa. Harry and I had saved his life. Now, it seemed, he was returning the favour.

"Hmm. And your evidence?" said Dr Sidding

"I have seen the Letter of Marque belonging to Harry Carter," said Walter in a clear and carrying voice. "It is not fiction as Major Dollard has stated. The Major is... misinformed."

"This isn't evidence!" fumed Major Dollard. "Surely you aren't taking the word of some common sailor above the word of an officer of His Majesty's Customs and Excise?"

Dr Sidding peered down his long nose.

"It is not a question of taking anyone's word but of what can – or can't – be proven," he said. "This man, an independent witness, has raised the possibility that a Letter of Marque from the government with permission to trade does exist. If it can be produced," he said, looking sternly at Harry, "then it will show that this man is not a smuggler but a duly appointed trader. If, however, the Letter of Marque cannot be produced, the penalty for smuggling at a time of war will be severe... most severe indeed."

"I assure you, sir," said Harry, "the Letter does exist. It is with my brother, an inn keeper near Penzance. I can send for it."

"Very well," said Dr Sidding. "My determination as to your guilt is adjourned for two weeks until the evidence can be produced. But I must warn you, should this fail to be forthcoming, my humour will have been most sorely tried. Yes, indeed."

"I won't let you down, sir," said Harry, who was positively beaming.

"This is outrageous!" bellowed Major Dollard. "This man is a notorious smuggler! He must be hanged at once!"

Dr Sidding's nose swelled dangerously at the Major's outburst.

"Must, sir? Must? May I remind you, sir, that you are in my Justice Room, that you have sworn as an Officer and a gentleman to uphold English law? Must me no musts, sir!"

Dollard was apoplectic. He couldn't believe that Harry and I had eluded him once again. But he hadn't given up yet.

"Then may I politely request, sir, that this felon be returned to gaol until such time – if such time occurs – that he can produce this famous Letter of Marque."

Dr Sidding paused.

"Your request is not unreasonable, Major Dollard. Mr Carter, you will be returned to prison to await the arrival of your documents. Take him down."

Harry's face collapsed, sinking from joy to despair in a single beat of his heart. Major Dollard had won after all – and England's future was lost.

To my surprise Walter winked at me with a slight smile on his face. Harry had missed the sign but a spark of hope had lit a flame of belief inside me: I felt sure that Walter had not been sent merely to lengthen our stay in the foul pit of Portsmouth prison – he must be here to help us.

The fight had gone out of Harry with Dr Sidding's verdict and the prison warders had to half carry him from the Justice Room. I trotted behind with a swagger and snapped my teeth at Major Dollard as I passed, making him curse and jump backwards. A small and petty revenge, but it was something.

Back inside our squalid cell, Harry sat slumped with his head in his hands. I, however, was aquiver with nervous energy and could barely keep my seat, pacing restlessly at the extremity of my rope, every nerve strained for the sound that would herald our return to freedom. I felt sure Walter would not let us down.

Time crawled by at an infuriatingly slow pace. My nerves were so taut I thought I would burst. Then I heard the voices of several men above: they were shouting orders at the prison warders. This was it! Our release – I was sure of it!

"Right! Let's be having you!" a rough voice shouted through the door. "All able bodied men to the front. You filthy lot have a chance to work off your sins in the King's Navy. This way! This way!"

It was the Press Gang that we had fled from just a few short hours before. They must have run out of people they could catch in the streets and had decided to empty the prisons instead. It wasn't quite the release I had expected, but Harry took his chance.

"Here!" he called. "Over here. I've been thirty-nine years at sea."

"This way then, lad," came the answer.

"I can't," yelled Harry. "I'm chained to the wall."

There was a muttered discussion outside.

"What are you in for, lad?"

"Smuggling!" yelled Harry.

There was further muffled discussion and the sound of a key in the rusty lock.

"All right, all right," said the recruiting man. "You come with us, lad, and you'll have a chance to repay your debt to society – and serve with the greatest Admiral as ever lived."

"I will!" said Harry, as they unchained him.

They started to march him away. Harry turned in panic as I yelped loudly.

"My dog! I must bring my dog!"

"Not in the Royal Navy, lad, you should know that," said the recruiting man roughly.

I howled.

"But she's a good ratter, sir. She'll keep us shipshape and clean, I promise you."

I barked and yanked desperately at the thick rope that restrained me.

"Not what you'd call a fearsome looking beast," said the man thoughtfully looking me up and down. "Oh all right then, bring her along, but if she's not as good as you say, she'll be walking the plank and thrown overboard before you can say 'Bonaparte'."

Together at last we stumbled into daylight along with a dozen sorry-looking creatures who had been dragged from the bowels of the prison.

The recruiting man didn't look too impressed with the others but was clearly pleased to have Harry, who was something of a gift, being strong, healthy and seaworthy. He examined Harry as if he were a prize bull.

I wanted to bear my teeth and show him that was no way to treat my saviour, but Harry stood there stoically, so I decided to bide my time. What was it that Dom Álvaro had said? Revenge is a dish best served cold.

We were marched down to the beach and stood in ragged ranks.

"Ahoy!" cried that happily familiar voice.

"Walter Abbot!" whispered Harry hoarsely.

"That man's for the Victory," said Walter to the recruiter, pointing at Harry.

"Says who?" said the recruiting man, pushing his ugly face into Walter's.

"Says me," said Walter menacingly. "The Admiral has asked for good men and good men is all I'll take. Hand him over."

The recruiter wasn't going to argue with a tough looking man like Walter or against the word of Nelson, and grudgingly conceded the point.

"All right, all right. He has to be signed up first and you is responsible for making sure he don't abscond."

Walter raised his eyebrows but agreed.

"Make your mark there," said the recruiter, pushing a ruled notebook in front of Harry.

Harry signed with a flourish – and was released.

Walter and Harry shook hands.

"I'm very happy to see you, Walter Abbot," said Harry. "I was feeling sorely wisht and wambling until I heard your voice in the Justice Room and again just now. How is that you are here?"

"Ah! I thought I caught the cut of your jib earlier but just as I was about to speak my piece, you was arrested for smuggling. Still keeping up the family business, Harry?" he whispered.

"I can't deny it," said Harry with a faint smile.

"And your Letter of Marque? Still got it?" asked Walter.

"Indeed! That 'tis all true!" said Harry.

"Ah well, not that it matters," said Walter, "you're a Navy man now."

Harry's face fell. "I can't join the Navy, Walter, I have important work to do."

Walter looked taken aback. "But you have signed up now; if you run, they'll track you down. Besides, I gave my word that you'd not abscond and I'll not have my word broken. The barge is waiting to take you aboard the Victory."

Harry chewed his lip.

"Very well," he said, "but you must do one more thing for me, Walter. I have important documents stored at my lodgings above the Black Dog tavern. Will you get them for me? I wouldn't ask but it's truly important – the Admiral will want to see what I have to show him."

Walter frowned. "I don't have much time. I have to be aboard before we weigh anchor for Spithead or they'll think I'm the one what has absconded. The tide is rising and I don't know the way to this tavern of yours."

I barked and wagged my tail.

"She'll show you!" said Harry pointing at me.

Walter looked somewhat sceptical but he couldn't refuse Harry's plea.

"Very well. I'll do this for you, Harry Carter, then you and I is even and I am in your debt no longer. 'Twill be all paid back. Agreed?"

They shook hands once more and Harry was marched away to the Victory's barge.

"And there's money to pay for the stabling of my horse!" called Harry over his shoulder.

Poor Cubert! I did not know how he would do in this sorry state of affairs.

Walter grumpily muttered to his fellow seamen that he'd make his own way aboard the Victory within the hour.

Watching Harry's departure with impotent fury from the harbour wall stood Dom Álvaro.

I was waiting impatiently to start our mission. I barked twice to show I was in a hurry. Walter frowned again but began to follow me through the busy streets.

I must have gone too fast for his slow seamen's legs because after a few minutes he shouted at me to wait. He leaned against a wall to catch his breath, his weathered face shiny with exertion.

I held my tongue and counted slowly, using all my paws – surely that was enough time for a person to rest! I barked again and pushed my head against his ankle to get him moving.

It is at such times that I wished I were the size of a bear and could bend humans to my will, but I am just a little thing and am often treated as such.

One of the reasons for my love and loyalty to Harry was that he treated all creatures the same, whether they crawled on the ground or flew in the air, whether they were the size of a snail or the height of an elephant (which I saw once at a circus in Ludgvan).

"Give me a breath," moaned Walter.

But I wouldn't. Time was too short and the mission too important. I barked urgently.

"All right, all right! Stop your mithering! I'm coming!"

He limped along behind me, weaving in and out of the human and animal traffic until we reached our lodgings.

I scampered up the stairs, past an indignant landlady who looked as if she intended to stop us, and Walter lumbered up behind me.

I stood by our door whining until he opened it.

"Who are you?!" screeched an elderly matron of astonishingly large proportions whose vast *derrière* was occupying the room. "Help! Help! I am to be ravished!"

"Nay, Madam!" gasped Walter, trying to catch his breath. "I have no such evil intention, I assure you."

"Oh. Well, what do you want?" she said in a much calmer manner.

"My friend, I mean, er..."

"Do speak out, young man, I don't have all day!" said the matron briskly.

"Ah, well," said Walter tugging aimlessly at his necktie.

I really thought a quick nip on the ankle might help him focus but instead I pawed the loose floorboard and gave a quick yip to draw him to the point.

"Ah, yes," he said again. "I was staying in this here room when I became embarrassed for ready money before sailing, you see. I'm with the Victory," he added proudly.

"Oh, you are one of the Admiral's brave souls," fluttered the lady in a quite different tone.

"Indeed, ma'am," said Walter, whose chest was swelling with pride. "And I had to vacate the premises in a bit of a hurry, the landlady being most particular about the settlement of bills..."

"Oh, but you are a hero," breathed the matron, "surely she could have been generous."

"Ah, no doubt she would," improvised Walter, "but I am not of that sort who would impose on a lady."

"No, I can tell that," murmured the matron. "You are a gentleman, sir, in every respect."

And do you know what? Walter blushed! He actually blushed. Really! I cannot account at all for the ways of humans. Especially when the matter was most pressing and the tide rising.

I barked sharply to bring him to the point once more.

"Yes, indeed," said Walter, blinking rapidly. "I hid some of my belongings beneath this loose board. Begging your pardon, but would you mind if I got 'em back."

"Of course not!" fluted the lady. "Please do. I shall avert my eyes."

"Oh, it's nothing like that!" said Walter blushing even more furiously... just some documents and whatnot."

He scrabbled around and managed to retrieve the crucial papers but managed to push Harry's purse quite out of reach. By this point I was astounded he still had the presence of mind to find anything during this hasty visit.

Walter stuffed the precious parchments, still wrapped in Harry's oilskin, into his shirt and we made our farewells.

"Might I know the name of the brave gentleman who risks his life to save the maids of England," whispered the matron.

"Walter Abbot of Honiton, ma'am."

"Well, Walter Abbot, I hope we shall meet again?" said the lady, gazing at him from beneath downcast lashes.

"God willing," said Walter with a husky voice. "God willing, my lady. Fare 'ee well."

He tiptoed from the room and closed the door quietly behind him.

"You may often find me here on market days," bawled the matron through the door.

I wondered if she had ever considered a career as a drill instructor in the army.

Walter's face had drained of all colour and he looked as white as if a bullet had buzzed past his ear.

He cleared his throat several times and stood as if moonstruck.

In the end I did give him a nip to remind him of his duty.

"Right!" he said. "Yes, time and tide wait for no man. Off we go, little maid, at the double."

He had quite forgot poor Cubert.

We ran back to the beach, ducking and diving through the press of humanity and caught the last supply barge leaving for the Victory.

Walter tucked me under one beefy arm and waded through the shallow waters, jumping aboard with practised ease.

I curled up on a pile of tarry ropes next to a dozen barrels of gunpowder. I lay very still for gunpowder does not make a reassuring travelling companion. But, I pondered, it might come in very useful should Bonaparte decide to face the might of the English fleet – and one small, black and white dog.

CHAPTER SIX

Aboard the Victory

Heart of oak are our ships, jolly tars are our men,
We always are ready; Steady, boys, steady!
We'll fight and we'll conquer again and again.

Official march of the Royal Navy

What a proud ship she was! My heart swelled at the sight of the Victory, readied for war, smart in fresh black and gold paint, her brass polished, her men eager for glory.

The ship was arranged like a huge floating castle, comprised of six main decks.

At the bottom of the ship, below the water line, was the hold. Here were stored six months worth of food and provisions for the entire crew – mostly salted beef, pork and ship's biscuit – and, therefore, it had become a favourite haunt of rats. I was happy to earn my keep ensuring that the rat population did not get out of hand, but was not happy to be always in darkness, rat hunting in the bowels of the ship. The hold smelled strongly of bilge water, stale air and rat droppings – and surely not as conducive to my good health as the clean air of my native Cornwall.

Water was stored in huge barrels called leaguers, each carrying some 150 gallons – big enough for Harry to bathe in – if he wanted to douse himself in water which over the coming months would gradually become foul and brackish and barely fit to drink.

One level above the hold was the orlop deck which was one of two main living areas for the sailors and marines. Each man was allotted between one-and-a-half and two feet in which they could hang the width of their hammocks. All the men swung together and the only privacy was in one's dreams.

It was not much room for a grown man and, squeezed in with Harry at night, there was little to be had of comfort for me. Most nights I lay along Harry's legs, keeping him warm, although he sometimes complained unkindly about my weight, even though it could hardly be called great.

Here, on this deck, the ship's surgeon, Mr William Beatty, kept his potions, lotions and packets of pills in a locked cabin. The orlop would also become the operating room in time of battle, being below the waterline and thus safe from enemy shot and shell. I hoped I would not be spending more time than necessary in that place.

I must admit I didn't like being below the waterline – it just wasn't natural. It reminded me of those Cornish mines that have shafts and tunnels dug beneath the sea. The miners dig down through the granite, following the seams of tin and copper. Where the valuable metal goes, the miners follow, even if this means tunnelling under the ocean's bedrock. Some say that the sound of pounding waves less than a fathom above one's head can drive a man near distraction and fill him with a maddening desire to feel the sun on his face again. I felt the same strong pangs of dislike and distrust on those lower decks of the Victory.

The magazines – gunpowder storerooms – were also on the orlop deck. To my mind another reason not to tarry nearby.

Above them was one of three gun decks and here, for the first time, evidence that the Victory was an instrument of war. And what an instrument! Thirty enormous cannon lined the sides of the ship. Each gun fired a ball of iron weighing 32 pounds – more than twice my weight. These terrible missiles could take off a man's head or dismast a ship or throw up cruel splinters of wood that sliced through flesh. In my imagination I thought I could hear the pounding of the guns in battle and shivered at the thought.

And yet this deck was also a second living area – the mess deck – for a large number of the ordinary seamen. At eight bells, which I called lunchtime, the mess cook would collect half of the daily ration of grog for his mess. The sailors lived their lives amongst the guns, these sullen reminders of the war, their enemies and their own mortality. It puzzled me greatly. Why do humans use their imaginations to create machines of such destructive power? I am only a small dog but sometimes I think that we beasts have more humanity in us than those who are said to be our betters and so more highly favoured by God.

Above was the middle gun deck which carried 28 cannon loaded with 24 pound cannonballs. It was also the wardroom or living area for the officers. I spent a lot of my time here because next to the wardroom was the galley – what landlubbers would call a kitchen. The location of the wardroom had two distinct advantages: officers would always get their food hot, unlike some of the poor crew; and I was always nearby at mealtimes to ensure that any intrepid rats did not taste the stew before the men. It was, by chance, also a good place for me to loiter as it ensured that many treats passed my way.

Two huge capstans sat squatly amongst the junior officers' quarters on that deck: they were used to raise and lower the two enormous anchors. It was an horrific sound as the massive metal chains rattled through when the anchors slipped into the sea –

many fathoms of heavy chain-links were used. I used to run when the order to raise or weigh anchor was given.

The upper gun deck carried 30 smaller cannon. I say 'smaller', but one of those iron cannonballs weighed about the same as me. It was also the deck where the senior officers had their slightly more comfortable and commodious quarters – rooms made private by the placing of wooden boards between them. Here was where the many skilled craftsmen worked their trade. Rope makers, sail makers, leather workers, carpenters – they all toiled in the flowing air and good light of this deck.

Above this was, at last, a fully open deck. The foc'sle was the area from which the sails were controlled. There were more cannon, of course – it made it impossible to forget that we were a ship of war and not a merchantman like Harry's little lugger.

The quarter deck was at the stern end and this was where the senior officers made their decisions and gave their orders – the beating heart at the centre of this wooden world. Lord Nelson could often be seen there, walking up and down, deep in thought.

He was a thoughtful man in more ways than one, as I came to learn.

His private cabin was behind the quarter deck and, it was rumoured, had a proper feather bed, not a hammock like the rest of the men. (I made it one of my earliest tasks to see if rumour were near the truth on this point.) But, curiously, for such a proud and jealous profession, the sailors did not begrudge the Admiral this small luxury but saw it instead as a just reward for a brave an honourable man. Indeed, they believed him to be their better and took pride in the small luxuries afforded by his cabin's fittings.

The upper deck also housed the great wheel by which the

Victory was steered. It took four sturdy men to turn the wheel during calm weather – and seven or eight when the weather turned squally, as it often did at this time of the year. A huge rope was wound around the wheel, passing down through two decks, where it was attached to the rudder that moved the Victory to port or starboard. If a ship had its rudder shot away during a battle it would drift around, crashing into any nearby ship or become a slave to the vagaries of the ocean's currents or until it ran aground. Either way, a rudderless ship was like a wingless bird and an easy target for enemy cannonball. The thought haunted the dreams of many a brave shipmate.

The wheel was somewhat protected by the small poop deck that partially covered it. The poop deck was a sort of raised viewing platform and signalling station. I have since learned that the word 'poop' means 'rear deck' in a foreign tongue. I think it odd that part of this great ship should be named by foreigners when it was foreigners that we were fighting. The ways of humans are very strange indeed.

But I liked the poop deck. From there I could find a quiet corner to sleep away a gentle hour or gaze through the shallow skylight into Nelson's private cabin and watch him at his work.

His manner never changed: he was calm and kind and courteous to all. But in those silent moments when only I watched him, unseen, unsuspected, unknown, I saw that the burdens of leadership weighed very greatly on him. More than once I heard him sigh and rest his quill, leaning his head in his hands, before taking up his writing as before. I don't think his brother officers saw the strain of his duty; indeed I believe My Lord had trained himself to conceal it as much as was humanly possible. But, I, being small and often disregarded, see things that others do not. I saw his suffering and my heart was heavy for his private burdens.

I had free access to every area of the ship from the hold to the poop deck. Not another soul on board learned the secrets of the Victory as I knew them. I began to feel that she was my ship – almost my home.

But that was in the early days, before we went to war. My feelings were to change greatly.

Harry, on the other hand, was confined to a much smaller area of the ship between the gun decks and it irked him. For all his life he was a man who had sailed his own course and been his own master. Now he was one of the lowest and the least and master of nothing.

The newly pressed men were not much trusted, although being Walter Abbot's friend brought Harry more esteem than would have been usual. His skill as a sailor was also apparent although the sheer scale of the Victory occasionally confounded him and the more experienced hands would pour good-natured scorn on his ham-handed efforts.

Although we had escaped from the foul confines of Portsmouth prison, Harry was not happy. It was simply not possible for him to reach Nelson. His rank was Ordinary Seaman and, as such, kept in check by the Able Seamen above him, such as Walter. Above them were the Leading Hands and their superiors were the Petty Officers and Warrant Officers. In other words, the full hierarchy of the Royal Navy meant that there was no chance whatsoever of Harry having an unsupervised moment in which to convey his urgent message to Lord Nelson.

His frustration grew daily. For one thing, we were sailing further away from home; and for another, Harry was convinced that we were sailing in the wrong direction.

He confided his concerns to me as we swung gently in our hammock that night.

"We are sailing West towards the Azores and yet we should be heading south towards the Spanish coast. But how can I get to my Lord to tell him?"

I licked his arm to give him a hint and he started at me thoughtfully.

"I would willingly give the papers to you, little maid," he said, "for I trust you with my very life. But the papers are large and you would be noticed and if noticed, stopped. I cannot risk these papers falling into the wrong hands – not after everything we have been through."

And with these troubled thoughts whirling around in his honest head, Harry spent a restless night tossing and turning.

I, on the other hand, slept soundly and companionably, listening to the creaking of the great ship and the steady beating of Harry's heart.

CHAPTER SEVEN

Lord Nelson

"It really is quite affecting to see the wonder and admiration and love and respect of the whole world; and the genuine expression of all these sentiments at once, from the gentle and simple the moment he is seen. It is beyond anything represented in a play or a poem of fame."

Lord Minto describing Horatio Nelson

We had been eight days on the Victory and Harry had still not been able to get close to Lord Nelson.

"I can't abear un!" said Harry softly as we swung gently to and fro in our hammock early the following morning. "To be so close and yet to be so far. How can I get near to him without having to go through the other officers? They seem like good enough men but I will trust only my Lord with these documents. Every passing day makes them more precious – and more pressing."

He raised his hand to his chest in an unconscious gesture. I knew that he had hidden the documents in his shirt, fearing to leave them unguarded during the day whilst we were at our work.

His kind face was furrowed in thought.

"I need to get close but cannot. Wait! I have it! I cannot get close but I know a small beast who can! Although you cannot carry the documents themselves, I will write my Lord a note and you will take it to him, little maid!"

I wagged my tail excitedly, happy to be able to help my dear friend.

Carefully, Harry tore a corner from the Reverend Grylls' translation and pencilled a brief note, then tucked it into my neckerchief with just enough showing so that Lord Nelson's curious mind would certainly seek it out.

"'Tis just gone four bells," said Harry, "and not many hours till dawn. I have to be about my business but you will find my Lord at his breakfast if you go now."

Harry lowered me from our hammock and I trotted through the mess deck as many sailors yawned and stretched, roused by the ringing of the great brass bell that tolled the hour, about to start their busy day. I scampered up the wooden ladders to the upper gun deck, two floors above.

Although I had every intention of delivering Harry's note without delay, an unforeseen problem forestalled me. Talented, I believe, at many things, I am simply not big enough to open doors.

I waited impatiently outside the Admiral's cabin until my Lord's steward entered with his morning coffee.

As soon as he opened the door I sped through his legs and with a single bound leaped onto my Lord's bed and woke him with a lick, which surprised him greatly.

"Out! Out!" yelled the steward who tried to shoo me from the bed.

But I crept up close to my Lord and nestled in the crook of his good arm.

"Whose dog is this?" said Nelson kindly. "Where did she come from?"

"She came aboard with us at Portsmouth, my Lord," said the steward. "She's the rat catcher for the cook."

"I'm sure you will do your duty well, little lass," said Nelson. "But happily my cabin is rat free at present, so be on your way and about your work."

I whined softy to show that this was not my intention at all and scratched at my neckerchief to draw his attention to it.

"Ugh! The dog must have fleas, my Lord!" said the steward with a tone of disgust. "I'll get rid of it at once."

"Wait one moment," said Nelson. "There appears to be a note tucked into her neckerchief."

He pulled out the corner of parchment and his face became serious.

"Where did you get this?" he said in a commanding voice. "Who is this Harry Carter?"

"He's one of the pressed men," said the steward in a worried tone. "It may be a plot – be careful, my Lord."

"I will be on deck at six bells," said Nelson. "I want this man brought to me – have him guarded closely until then."

This was not at all what I had expected. I was severely taken aback at this unexpected reversal in our fortunes.

The steward called the captain of marines and four burly men. They hastened to obey, their weapons held with bayonets fixed. They encircled Harry as he ate his breakfast of ship's biscuit and peas on the mess deck.

"What's all this clitter?" said Walter Abbot looking from me to Harry with a bemused expression on his face.

"Quiet!" ordered the marine captain. "This man, Harry Carter, is wanted above by his Lordship. 'Tis serious, lad, so at the double."

Poor Harry was taken from his breakfast and, guarded by the four marines with muskets he was dragged onto the quarter deck very roughly.

With a cold sensation in my heart I realised that they suspected Harry as some sort of assassin, sent to bring down the greatest Admiral as ever lived. Indeed, they thought Harry was some sort of spy and his note a ploy to get my Lord alone and commit murder!

I just hoped they would give Harry a chance to hand the documents to my Lord and prove his innocence – and his loyalty.

Dawn was late coming at this time of year and the moon still glowed wearily in the sky when Harry was brought in front of my Lord Nelson.

"What is your name?" said Nelson.

"Harry Carter."

"You are a pressed man?" said my Lord.

"Yes, but..."

"Answer 'yes' or 'no'," shouted one of the junior officers.

Harry shook off his restraining hand.

"My Lord!" said Harry urgently. "I must speak frankly with you!"

There was a surprised intake of breath from all around and several of the officers looked furious that Harry had dared to approach his master and speak in this manner.

I trotted over to Harry and sat down next to him, mutely giving my assurance that Harry was a good man and one to be trusted.

Nelson, however, merely swept his one good eye across Harry, resting briefly on me. He must not have been displeased with what he saw because he replied,

"You may speak, Mr Carter."

"I have been trying to speak to you, my Lord, for eight days," said Harry desperately. "My dog and I travelled a brah way to find you – from near Penzance, my Lord. I must deliver these papers to you. I daresn't give them to no other."

Harry pulled the Spanish parchment and the Reverend Grylls' translation from his shirt and thrust them towards Nelson.

Captain Hardy took them from him and unfolded the papers, holding them for Nelson to read.

Nelson frowned slightly and his mouth drew into a tight line as he rapidly studied both sets of papers.

"How did you come by these documents? Speak, man!"

I could tell that it was a great relief to Harry to finally speak of the events of so many nights ago and to unburden himself to the man who could and would take action.

Harry described the shipwreck at the cliffs below our village, our journey to Portsmouth, our imprisonment and escape. I must admit, it sounded as exciting as a novel.

"And so you see, my Lord," finished Harry, "I thought you should know what these papers tell."

"You were right," said Nelson. "Have you told the contents of these papers to anyone? Anyone other than the good Reverend who translated them?"

Harry's cheeks burned with a dull red.

"Come, come, man! To whom did you convey this information? Be plain! It is vital!"

Harry cast a worried glance at me and I pushed my nose against his leg so he knew that I was there supporting him.

"I... I told my dog, sir!" said Harry at last.

"Your dog? You told your dog?" said Nelson, his mouth twitching slightly.

"Yes, sir," said Harry, staring at the deck.

"And... your dog is a good, loyal Cornish lass who would not have traded this information for, say... a bacon sandwich?"

"She's as loyal as they come!" said Harry stoutly. "She's told no-one; I'd bet my life on it."

"I am glad to hear it," said Nelson seriously.

The officers around the Admiral began to smile and the ripples of laughter spread across the deck like an evening tide.

The realisation slowly dawned on Harry that Lord Nelson had been pulling his leg, ever so gently. He smiled sheepishly.

"Thank you, sir," he muttered.

"No, no. It is I who must thank you," said Nelson, clapping his good hand on Harry's shoulder, "you and your fine dog. You have both of you done a great service to your country; greater than most men will ever know. England owes you a debt, my friend, and Cornwall a greater one."

"So, gentleman," he said, addressing his fellow officers. "The French have hoodwinked us. The invasion flotilla is to come from Spain, not France and the fleet is not anchored among the Caribbean islands. This information changes everything, gentlemen. From this moment we, Bonaparte's constant opponent, will change our course and head to the southernmost tip of Spain, to Cape Trafalgar – and to War."

———⊷•⊶———

Sailing south, we passed Lisbon on the Portuguese coast and travelled on towards Cape Saint Vincent and Spain.

The following day, some 40 miles offshore from the great Spanish maritime city of Cadiz, we dropped anchor. The French and Spanish fleets were massed in the safety of the harbour just as Harry's documents had foretold. We were, at last, within a short distance of our foe. And it was here that we celebrated the Admiral's birthday. He was 47 years old although he looked older, being much careworn by life and loss, and by his position as Vice-Admiral and leader of the fleet.

In a festive mood, the decks were scrubbed with seawater, as were many of the men. I hid behind the poop deck until the mania for bathing had passed.

Several of the hands with the sweetest voices had got up a choir and serenaded my Lord with a selection of sea-shanties and popular songs of home. I howled along with the rest and got the biggest cheer of the day, which annoyed some members of the choir, though whyfore I knew not.

The cook, Mr Carroll, had been sweating long hours in the galley, aided by Nelson's steward and several of the cleaner looking sailors, to produce a celebration meal of astonishing variety and quality from such cramped and unprepossessing conditions.

As the evening drew in, barges from the rest of the fleet began to bring the captains of the other ships of the fleet to the Victory to dine in style and drink the health of the Admiral.

Dish after dish of astonishingly-scented food issued forth from the kitchen: mackerel, rabbit, pheasant, chicken, pork chops, something spicy I couldn't identify and baskets of brightly-coloured fruits followed a steaming suet pudding. Each course was accompanied by a different case of wine. Mr Carroll had clearly been planning this celebration since before we ever left Portsmouth harbour. I licked my lips a great deal, I can tell you.

The rest of the crew were not forgot and had their share, receiving a large helping of salted pork and peas and an extra ration of rum with which they toasted their leader, heaping increasingly violent imprecations on the head of Bonaparte. Such fine men! On an evening as this I felt sure that the French would run at the merest sight of our fine fleet. Such naivety may be forgiven, I hope, such was the fervour and joyous celebration of that night.

Harry, in particular, enjoyed the occasion. He had become something of a hero when it became known the role that he had played in leading us into battle. His health was drunk and his back was slapped and many times he was asked to repeat the story of our escape from Major Dollard and the part played, therein, by our dear Walter Abbot. Adding to the general joyous nature of the occasion were the many and ingenious punishments that were to be devised for Major Dollard should he ever be foolhardy enough to come near a Victory man, or his dog.

When the party reached its zenith I crept away. I am not, nor never have been, a creature who enjoys a deal of noise, however kindly meant. I made my way to the Admiral's cabin where celebrations of a gentler nature were taking place.

The steward, Mr Spedillo, had become a kindly friend once he was certain I was beloved of his Lordship. He opened the door for me and surreptitiously dropped half a pork chop on the floor next to me. I ate it gratefully, licking every morsel and drop of gravy from my lips. He leaned down to stroke me.

"There will be much rich food for you, leetle lady," he said in his strange, sing-song accent. "Mind your manners, don't wolf your food and you'll do well."

I thanked him with a lick and trotted in.

Some eyebrows were raised at my appearance but because my Lord simply rested his good hand on my head in companionable silence, nothing was said.

Around the mahogany table sat men whose names were soon to become legend amongst the people of Britain.

My Lord sat at the head of the table, as befitted his rank. Next to him sat Captain Hardy and Mr Beatty, the Surgeon, his dearest friends aboard. On his other side sat Vice-Admiral Collingwood of the Royal Sovereign, and Captain Henry Blackwood of the Euraylus, the senior frigate captain. He was flanked by Captain Fremantle of the Neptune, Captain Duff of the Mars and Captain Hargood of the Belleisle.

The happy chatter of naval men rang in my ears and I curled up most contentedly in a corner of the cabin, seemingly asleep but in fact listening to every word.

As the port wine circled the table in a clockwise direction, as was proper, and the fug of pipe smoke thickened, Nelson rose to his feet. The conversation died immediately and my Admiral, the smallest man in the room, commanded the greatest attention.

"Gentlemen," he said, "the time has come to talk of war."

Every pair of eyes in the room was directed towards Nelson's pale and serious face.

"I have been thinking long and hard about how we can – how we will – defeat Bonaparte. It will be no easy task. Our opponent and leader of the French fleet, Admiral Villeneuve, is no fool but with courage, skill, audacity and daring, we will prevail."

The room was silent.

"I have a new plan of attack and it is this. The usual means of fighting is to run our fleet in a line of ships parallel to that of the enemy, trading broadside after broadside with our cannon. As I say, that is the usual way, but it is not my way. Instead I will lead one half of the fleet at right angles to the French line; Vice-Admiral Collingwood will lead the second column. We will drive these two wedges into the French fleet, causing panic and chaos. Then, gentlemen, we will be amongst them like wolves, bringing down ship after ship. And in case my signal flags can neither be seen nor perfectly understood, no captain can do very wrong if he places his ship alongside that of an enemy."

A shocked silence followed that statement.

"But, sir!" said one young officer, braver – or more foolhardy – than the rest. "But, sir! Whilst we cut across the French line we will be unable to aim our guns at them; the French will be able to send shot after shot into us; we will be cut to pieces before we can come alongside of them and fire our own guns. The first two ships will be especially at risk."

It seemed to me that the officer had fixed on the weak point of the plan. I blinked in surprise: I had not thought that my Lord had weak points.

Whether it was a trick of the candle light, I could not say, but my Lord's good eye gleamed with the certainty of the converted.

"The first ship indeed will take a pummelling but what glory will fall on them! This plan will work, gentlemen, because it is risky, because it is audacious, and because it has never been done before. It will be the last thing the French expect. And because of this we will have the upper hand of surprise – and we will win."

Vice-Admiral Collingwood raised his eyes to meet Nelson's, a slight smile playing about his lips.

"It is most singular," he said. "Most singular – and most simple. Should the French ever decide to leave the safety of Cadiz harbour and allow us to get at them, it must succeed. You are, Horatio, surrounded by friends whom you inspire with confidence."

He raised his glass: "To the Nelson Touch! And a lasting and glorious Peace our reward!"

His brother officers stood and raised their glasses and huzzahed him over and over again.

I wagged my tail with my whole body, determined to join the salute to a brave and audacious man.

The drinking and toasting lasted long into the night and I fell asleep with the sound of victory ringing in my ears.

CHAPTER EIGHT

England expects every man (and dog) to do his duty

"May the great God, whom I worship, grant to my country and for the benefit of Europe in general, a great and glorious victory: and may no misconduct, in anyone, tarnish it: and may humanity after victory be the predominant feature in the British Fleet. For myself Individually, I commit my life to Him who made me and may His blessing light upon my endeavours for serving my Country faithfully. To Him I resign myself and the just cause which is entrusted to me to defend. Amen, Amen, Amen."

Horatio Nelson, the morning of 21st October, 1805

And then we waited. Day after tedious day passed on board the Victory with our anchors firmly sunk, unmoving, in the seas off the coast of Cadiz.

No-one could understand why Bonaparte's fleet did neither fight nor flee. Nelson had designed to leave them an escape route hoping and believing that they would take it, rather than risk being pinned in Cadiz and attacked with fire ships – ships deliberately set alight and sailed into the harbour – a move that would be catastrophic for the enemy. And yet, they stayed their hand.

We waited.

"It's all a meesy-y-mazy confusion, little maid," said Harry, scratching his honest head. "Why won't the Frenchies fight?"

"Would you," said Walter, "if you knew the greatest Admiral as ever lived was waiting to blow you to smithereens?"

"There's truth in your words, Walter," said Harry. "But it's a loagy nuisance and no mistake."

I had my mouth full of dead rat at the time, or I would have barked my agreement: instead I wagged my tail vociferously.

I had spent so much time in the hold clearing out the rat population over the last few dull days that it hardly seemed fair to continue with my work, such a sport had I made of it. Instead I preferred to waste many an hour watching my Lord from the poop deck or lying by his feet whilst he wrote his letters.

I caught the odd rat simply to show I had not forgot my duty and, as Napoleon himself would say, *pour encourager les autres.*

Nelson, too, longed for action, I knew. He prayed for some conclusion to this long, drawn out game of warfare.

"Ah, little lass," he said one day as he looked up from his desk and spotted me lounging on the poop deck. "If only Villeneuve would act, then we might all go home: you and Harry to your Cornish cottage and me to my little paradise in Merton with my dear Emma and our darling little daughter Horatia. I wish nothing more than for this business to be over so that I might see my family again, as must you."

He stretched his back and rubbed the shoulder where his right arm should have been. He sighed and shook his head slowly.

"Duty must come first."

It didn't seem kind to point out that whilst I was with Harry I had my family with me, but it was true that I longed to see the white beaches and black cliffs of Cornwall again.

To raise the morale of his bored fleet, my Lord ordered that every ship be painted with broad black and yellow stripes to match the Victory. It was a source of great pride to the crew that their ships displayed the equipage of their Admiral. The men of the Victory were not so enamoured, however.

"I don't see why every Jack Tar should have these stinging colours," said Walter Abbott. "They're not the ones carrying Lord Nelson."

"Come, come now, Walter," said Harry mildly. "You miss the hand there. My Lord wishes to honour all the men of his fleet. They will look to us in battle – and wearing his colours 'twill raise their spirits. You mun see the point of that."

It occurred to me that it would be a good thing to be easily recognisable by a friendly ship during a battle; I did not wish to sink to Davy Jones' Locker because of a misunderstanding and a touch of friendly fire.

"Harrumph," said Walter, neither agreeing nor disagreeing. "I just wish those Frenchies would come out and face us."

We all agreed with that.

But it seemed that my Lord's wish – and ours – for an end to this dreary inactivity was to be granted because early the next morning, the 19th October, Bonaparte's grand fleet finally fled Cadiz.

It was Saturday and the wind was squally and blew unevenly. Harry grimaced at the sails flapping haphazardly.

"These scamp winds do us no good," he said, a worried tone in his voice.

"Aye," agreed Walter, "but they'll not help the Frenchies either and who's the better sailors, them or us, I'd like to know."

"True, true," replied Harry. "The Admiral will see us right. But 'tis now or never for this weather will break soon."

We all gazed anxiously at the sky. The experienced seadogs

amongst us recognised that an ominous western swell meant a storm was coming, one that would scatter the two fleets like so many poppy seeds. Then our chance of destroying the French would be gone until the Spring, and who knew what chances and choices another year might bring.

The wind blew strongly all day and every spare second they had, the men would stare at the sky and the scudding clouds, wishing and wondering and waiting. The weekend dragged by. I spent most of my time hidden in my secret hidey-hole on the poop deck, looking down into Nelson's cabin. He would be the one who made the decision – and my patient study meant that I would be the first to know it!

Early on Monday morning I had taken up my position as usual, curled up in a comfortable loop of rope. I could see my Lord writing at his desk. From his expression I could tell that he was writing to his beloved Emma. A knock at the door left his letter unfinished.

It was the Signal Lieutenant with a message.

"Yes, Mr Pasco?" said Nelson laying down his quill and looking up.

"It's a message from Admiral Collingwood, sir," said the young officer.

"Please read it."

"It says: 'The enemy are going to fight', sir."

It was the message we had all been waiting for. I gaped open mouthed at my Lord and peered further in so as not to miss a syllable of what passed.

A grim expression of determination played across Nelson's face. "Thank you, Mr Pasco. Have this message sent to the rest of the fleet..."

He raised his eyes in thought, preparing his words carefully, and happened to espy me. I wagged my tail and he smiled gently.

"Yes, send this message: 'England expects every man – and dog – to do his duty'."

The young officer looked up, surprised.

"'And dog', sir?"

"Yes, Mr Pasco," said my Lord giving him a long look that brooked no discussion. "'And dog'."

The Signal Lieutenant glanced up at me but thought better of speaking his mind. He scratched the Admiral's words into his notebook then hurried to the quarter deck to send the message to the rest of the fleet with a display of colourful flags. Nelson summoned his steward and dressed carefully in his Admiral's uniform of dark blue coat, decorated with silver stars and golden buttons. Placing his bicorne hat carefully on his tidy hair, he followed at a more leisurely pace. I scampered down from the poop deck to find Harry.

Word had spread quickly amongst the crew as the signal flags fluttered gaily above us. Every sailor, marine, cook and ship's boy knew that it was an hour of great moment; we all knew that the enemy had fled and that we would give chase, that we were in fact, about to face Bonaparte's fleet at last.

The three gun decks were cleared for action, an air of barely checked anticipation amongst the crew.

Once the cannon, the machines of war, were in place, there were other, more private preparations to be made. The men carefully stowed away what few personal possessions they held dear: a letter from home, a lock of hair, a prayer book or bottle of rum. The rolled hammocks and bedding were stuffed into the netting along the side of the ship to offer some protection against the shower of wooden splinters that would soon rain down on our heads.

The officers' fine furniture was packed away and moved down to the lower decks; the squawking chickens were also taken below. I hoped I had killed enough rats to offer the poor creatures a chance of survival. The darkness and coming noise was sure to put them off their laying for weeks – if any of us survived that long.

Those men who could write were kept busy by their friends and fellow sailors scribbling farewell notes to their nearest and dearest, in case this day was to be their last.

I noticed for the first time how young were some of the crew. Cornelius Carroll, son of the cook was 12; William Huchinson, Henry Lancaster and Hugh Portfield were all just 14 years of age – and yet today they had the faces of old men.

"Will you write me a note to my mam, Harry?" said Hugh.

"That I will, lad," said Harry.

He pulled out his small notebook, licked the stub of his pencil and waited.

Hugh screwed up his eyes in concentration. Like most of the men, words were not his strong point.

"Dearest Mam," he said at last. "I never had much learning, though 'twas not your fault, so Harry, my friend, is writing this for me. The enemy have run for it and the waiting is over. The Victory is a fine ship with a fine crew. If I don't see tomorrow's morning, I leave all my wages what is owing to you, mam, my penknife and best shirt which you can sell to help with bringing up my sisters. I'm sorry you had to manage the farm alone but a life at sea was the life for me. Please forgive me and pray for my eternal soul, what you told me once I surely had. Your loving son, Hugh Portfield."

He looked anxiously at Harry. "Do you think that's all right,

Harry?" he said.

Harry nodded slowly and cleared his throat before he spoke. "'Tis a fine letter for any boy to send his mother. But Lord willing, 'twill not be needed this day or any day soon."

"I hope I don't get hurt," said Hugh. "I'd rather die than lose a leg for then I'll be a cripple and no use to anyone."

"Now listen here, boy," said Harry roughly. "Our fleet is led by a man with one arm – a cripple, if you like. Is he less of a man for having just one arm and good sight in one eye? No! He is the biggest man you'll ever meet."

Hugh hung his head. Harry clapped his hand on the boy's shoulder and only I saw him wipe a tear from his eye. Harry never could bear to see a fellow creature in pain.

Silently, he collected the letters, last wills and testaments and handed them to a young Midshipman for safe keeping. I wondered what he had written in his own epitaph. I had only one wish, and that was to be with Harry, come what may – although I should have liked to have seen Cornwall one more time.

That morning we had a proper breakfast, fit for fighting men and their dog. Instead of the usual mess of burgoo, a spicy stew of indeterminate meat and vegetables, my Lord ordered that the men should have fresh bread, cheese, butter and beer. This was a tremendous treat and Harry stared at his half a loaf as if it were the most beautiful sight he had ever seen. Of course I was used to eating well, spending many mealtimes with my Lord Nelson and the other officers. In fact if truth be told, I had several more meals a day than I was supposed to, which accounted for my well-filled curves and sleek coat. Even so, Harry shared a part of his feast with me, and I accepted a crumb or two, just to be sociable. All save the beer, which I could not abide.

Some of the men picked up their instruments and played a jaunty tune, much at odds with the way we all felt, but rousing to our spirits nonetheless.

Then we paraded on deck, as smart as new shillings, and Nelson looked every man in the eye to let him know we were all equally valued this day.

I stretched myself to my greatest height, which is not so very much, if truth be told, and held my tail as upright as a flagpole.

"Your dog stands to attention," said the Admiral when he reached Harry.

"That she does," said Harry, "for she is a brave, Cornish dog and fights for her country, as do I."

A ripple of amusement ran across the deck, but Harry and I were parading for our Admiral; neither of us moved a muscle.

Nelson nodded slowly then said,

"Look after her, Mr Carter. She is a fine beast indeed."

My heart swelled with such pride that I thought my chest should burst.

——◈——

Inexplicably, the wind had dropped to the faintest breath, like a long, drawn out sigh.

We weighed anchor with an ear-splitting churning of metal as the huge chains were slowly wound up by the capstans.

The Victory began to move, as if a leviathan of the deep had been roused from its slumber. A shiver ran through me and I looked fearfully at Harry. His face was set and grim; he had no words to comfort me but picked me up and held me close as if fearing it would be for the last time. I snuggled into him, smelling the salt and sweat.

Captain Blackwood, Nelson's devoted friend prepared to depart to command his own ship. He saluted my Lord and, trying to speak cheerfully, saying:

"I trust I will return this afternoon, my Lord, to find that you have taken 20 ships!"

Nelson grasped him by the hand and looked into his eyes.

"God bless you, Blackwood: but I shall never speak to you again."

There was an audible gasp. What did he mean?

I do not think my Lord had meant to be cruel but I could not bear the look of shock and pain on Captain Blackwood's face. He didn't know what he had done to earn such a harsh send off. The mood on the Victory hardened.

A new set of signal flags was hoisted aloft to flutter merrily in the light breeze: 'Engage the enemy more closely'.

The Victory's wooden bulk moved forward.

Half a mile to our south Vice-Admiral Collingwood also moved to engage the enemy. His ship Royal Sovereign had been recently re-fitted with a splendid new copper hull. The shining metal cut through the water making good time, speeding ahead of the Victory and the rest of our fleet.

The enemy were primed and ready and I trembled for Collingwood's crew.

I saw the powder flash of a dozen French and Spanish cannon and a tremendous booming sound echoed across the water. The Royal Sovereign shuddered as a wicked hail of iron balls shredded her stout timbers. In my mind's eye I could see the carnage that had surely met them.

This was the most dangerous time for Nelson's fleet: still some distance from the enemy and no English ship yet in a position to return fire. We could only watch and wait and endure.

The Royal Sovereign inched her way forward into the ferocious fire power of a hundred cannon. As she moved nearer into the hail of hot metal, every enemy shot was beginning to tell and the poor ship seemed to quiver with pain.

I could only imagine what hellish scenes were taking place on her deck and yet I knew that I would not need imagination for much longer.

Nelson, however, was jubilant at seeing his plan so bravely carried into action:

"See," he said, pointing to the Royal Sovereign. "See how that noble fellow Collingwood carries his ship into action!"

The slightest breath of air filled the sails and carried us gently forwards. As we crept nearer, I saw the black, yawning mouths of what seemed like a thousand cannon trained on us.

It was not long before it was we who sailed into action and under heavy fire.

Slowly, so slowly, the light airs took us towards the enemy. Then their guns opened, as if of one accord, of one devilish mind.

B-BOOM! Heavy shot crashed into the bow of the Victory and I jumped in shock, my ears assaulted by the violent noise and thunder beneath my paws.

"Time to take cover now, little maid," shouted Harry over the fury of the guns. "Get below decks – 'twill be safer for you there. I couldn't a bear-un if anything should happen to you!"

But I was transfixed. I had resolved not to leave Harry. How could I go below decks, not knowing what his fate might be? Instead I crept into a corner of the exposed quarterdeck where I was least likely be trodden on. Among the many hazards, this was a very real one, for who there had time to notice a small dog beneath their frantic feet?

From this small vantage point, I could see both Harry and my Lord: Harry was working the rigging, trying to get the maximum wind-power from the gentle breeze; and Lord Nelson defied the enemy by pacing up and down the deck, in full uniform, his blue coat bright with stars and medals. He was in plain view of the French snipers but his presence gave the men heart, as was his intent, no matter the possible cost to himself. That's what made him the leader that men would follow into hell and back.

Then iron balls and chain shot rained down on our rigging, trying to tear it to pieces and halt our onward progress. Harry had his work cut out ensuring that the sails were used to their best efficiency whilst scything through damaged lines and replacing them, where he could, with fresh rope. It was hot work indeed.

Everywhere was noise but full of purpose. Then a man's scream pierced the volley of shot and I saw Nelson's aide, John Scott, cut in two by a cannonball. My Lord's face was white but calm as he oversaw poor John Scott's remains tossed into the sea. Sand was scattered to cover the bloody spot on the deck where a man had once stood; blood is very slippery, especially in great quantity. Such scenes were repeated endlessly across our bold fleet.

There was no time to mourn and worse was to come.

A clever shot – or a lucky one – smashed through the great wheel that steered the Victory. This could have been a serious problem but my Lord merely ordered the ship to be steered using the great ropes on the lower decks that were still attached to the rudder. Shouted orders were relayed by a team as 20 men steered the huge rudder and we ploughed onwards into the maelstrom of battle.

As the iron shot struck the deck and sides of the ship, huge splinters were thrown up. One took the buckle right off Captain Hardy's shoe but the gentleman himself was unhurt. Others were less lucky, and the splinters flew like arrows. I cowered in my corner, afraid to look, afraid to look away.

My Lord glanced over to check that Captain Hardy was unhurt and cheeringly commented, "This is too warm work to last for long".

I hoped rather than believed he was right. I did not understand how men could stand so calmly whilst death rained through the air: every impulse in my small body urged me to run. But where to? Nowhere was safe. I suppose I could have hidden in the hold with the rats but I would not then know what became of my friends – and I could not leave them. All I could do was wait and watch – and pray that God would be merciful this day.

But God was elsewhere. Perhaps he could not to bear to look upon what he had created. I saw the small, limp body of Hugh Portfield thrown over the side of Victory with many others. The sea was red with blood and the bodies swirled around us in obscene shoals. I wondered what watery grave his earthly remains would find.

In all this time we had not yet fired a single shot. The men had soaked up more punishment than I had thought humanly possible and they were in a ferocious mood.

Shortly after noon the command finally rang across the deck, "Make ready to fire!"

At last our own guns engaged the enemy. It was a relief to be able to return fire but the noise! The very air trembled at the sound and I felt rather than heard each powder charge explode from 50 double-shotted broadside guns with lethal force. The enemy sailors were mown down like so many stalks of wheat during the harvest. But what a harvest: we were so close to the French and Spanish ships that I could see the faces of the enemy we fought – men and boys just like those on the Victory. Why did we fight? For the King? For freedom? I could not answer the question: I simply knew that we fought for England, for Cornwall, for our homes. And I, if I could be said to have fought at all, I fought for my family – I fought for Harry.

Our deadly close-quarter assault had killed over 200 enemy and disabled 28 of their guns. Only Admiral Villeneuve still stood on his deck, surrounded by the dead and dying. What must he have felt? I could not, nor would not, guess.

We had blasted our way through the French and Spanish line but now we were boxed in and fighting on three sides. We had one card left to play – but it was a desperate one indeed.

Captain Hardy was given permission to ram the Victory into the side of a French ship, the Redoubtable. It was a bold manoeuvre but one that would leave us exposed and vulnerable. But if it worked...

The force of the collision knocked many men from their feet. I saw Harry thrown from the rigging and crash down onto the deck. I ran towards him but he was unmoving. I barked urgently and a smoke-blackened sailor knelt beside him.

"Out cold, but not dead," he muttered.

I was distraught! To see my friend laid low – it was one of the worst moments of my life. The sailor dragged Harry across the deck and laid him next to the remains of the great wheel where he might be afforded some small shelter from the violence of battle. It was not much but my heart went out to the stranger who could show kindness at such a time.

The continuing shriek of splintering wood tore the air. The

Redoubtable shuddered and lurched as we rammed into her, tonnes and tonnes of wood ploughing onwards, unstoppable, inhuman.

We could not escape, we could not signal for help, our rigging being completely destroyed. We continued to fight as best we could but we were overwhelmed by the enemy.

We prepared to be boarded.

Victory was pinned fast, grinding wood against wood of the French ship. Musket shot and grenades lashed the deck as the enemy prepared themselves for the assault. Our battle would now be close at hand.

But something miraculous had happened – the fight had quite gone out of the enemy. Something stayed their hand and the expected shower of grappling hooks and boarders did not appear.

Despite Victory's predicament, Nelson's tactics had worked: the French and Spanish were shocked at the brutality of the attack and the unexpected change of battle formation.

We were wreathed in the smoke of a thousand guns and the air smelled sulphurous from gunpowder. Hell itself could not be so very different, I thought.

I glanced up at Nelson and he halted his constant pacing to smile at me.

A shot rang out.

A look of surprise crossed Nelson's face; then he fell to his knees.

A slow stain of red appeared on his blue coat. Nelson looked down. He seemed more surprised than fearful.

I bounded towards him and felt rather than saw the explosion that knocked me sideways. A hand grenade had landed on the deck a few paces away. I never knew the name of the man who saved my life: one minute he was there and the next he was a memory and mist of flesh. I was astonished to see a bloom of red blood on my white fur. I thought it must be his, the stranger's. And then my legs gave way and pain flooded through me. I had been hit with a piece of shrapnel, a small part of which was lodged between my ribs.

I whimpered once and collapsed next to my Lord.

Captain Hardy and two other sailors rushed up.

"Get him to the surgeon!" roared Captain Hardy. "Now!"

"Wait!" said Nelson softly. "Bring the dog, too."

"But my Lord!" cried Hardy.

"Her life is worth something, as well," said Nelson in gentle reprimand.

"Very well," replied Captain Hardy, his face grey with worry. "Take them both."

Careful hands carried us from the sunlight to the surgeon below decks. He was already hard at work, his apron stiff with gore from his grim business, and then he saw that his dear friend was before him.

"Oh my dear sir!" cried Mr Beatty. "What have they done to you?"

"They have done for me at last, my backbone is shot through," replied the Admiral in a calm voice.

I could smell the salt of blood in the air and the cries of the wretched wounded filled my ears.

"I'm done for, William," said Nelson with a slight smile. "Promise me they'll look after Emma and little Horatia, won't you? There's nothing you can do for me."

Mr Beatty refused to believe this could be true but his expert surgeon's eye soon saw that the only comfort for Nelson was to let him die in peace, and he still had much work to do.

"You have men to save, Mr Beatty," commanded my Lord. "And this small dog, if you please. She is rather dear to me and has given me much comfort these past weeks."

Without further question, the surgeon pulled the piece of iron from my side, thrust a few hasty stitches through my torn skin and washed the wound with seawater. Then he bound me with a small rag of clean linen and laid me down so my Lord could reach me with his good hand. It hurt me to wag my tail but I did it for him.

We lay together quietly and I was soothed by the faltering beat of his noble heart. Even with so little time there were no words to pass between us.

It was infernally hot and I was aware of a raging thirst as I dipped in and out of a waking nightmare.

One of the powder monkeys, the young boys who loaded the cannon, had lost two fingers and part of his ear. As soon as Mr Beatty had bound up his damaged hand and staunched the flow

of blood from his head, the boy hurried to get a drink for Lord Nelson. The smell of sweet lemonade made my nostrils twitch. It seemed so unlikely that I wondered, confused, if I were back home in Cornwall, at the church picnic on a bright summer's day.

The boy helped my Lord to drink and then poured a few drops into my mouth. The sweet liquid brought me back to consciousness and I lay peacefully as the great guns shuddered and raged above me.

"I'm dying, little Pip," said Nelson softly. "I feel nothing below my chest and soon I will feel nothing at all. Within the hour I will be on the greatest adventure of them all; you, I pray, will soon be safely home in your beloved Cornwall."

Then Captain Hardy's voice was echoing through the deck and his large frame was silhouetted against the flickering light of candles.

Nelson raised his eyes to those of his dear friend.

"We have pushed the French into retreat, my Lord," said Hardy, his voice hoarse with emotion. "Villeneuve has surrendered. The rest of Bonaparte's fleet will soon do the same. You have won!"

Nelson tried to raise his hand to Captain Hardy, but it fell limply at his side. He looked very frail.

He lay with his eyes closed, summoning his energy to speak.

"There's a storm coming," he said. "I can feel it still. You must have the anchors lowered or we'll lose many ships."

Hardy's lips twisted into a brief smile.

"Of course. I'll send a message to Admiral Collingwood. But don't worry about that now. You have to save your energy on recovering, Horatio."

Nelson shook his head tiredly.

"I'm quite done for. But I have one last request – I wish to be buried on English soil, not at sea. Will you see to that for me?"

"My dear Horatio, I will see that it is done."

The Captain knelt down beside the dying man, kissed him briefly on his ashen cheek and held his hand.

"Kismet, Hardy," whispered Nelson.

There was nothing else to say.

Then with tears falling down his face Captain Hardy went back to the job of finishing what Bonaparte had started. He had his work to do, as we had done ours.

The chaplain, Mr Scott, crouched down next to my Lord and prayed in the darkness.

I think it comforted Nelson because he smiled once and said,

"Thank God I have done my duty."

And then he died.

CHAPTER NINE

Cape Trafalgar Storm

A canine hero is our Pip
Famed for exploits on land and ship.

Cornish folk song (Brian Harris)

The last of the enemy surrendered at 4.30pm that day, but I knew nothing of it.

The cost of victory was high: seventeen-hundred English were killed or wounded, and some six thousand of the enemy were in the same pitiable condition. Several ships had sunk and many were beyond repair; the sea was red with blood. Mangled bodies floated in small groups like some nightmarish shoal of fish.

I lay next to Lord Nelson's body for what seemed like an eternity, although it was certainly only a few hours.

His body had been covered with a white sheet that slowly turned dark with his blood. It had been his final wish that he be buried on English soil and his wish would be obeyed.

Two sailors and two marines came for my Lord's mortal remains. They wrapped him in a winding sheet and placed him in a barrel of his favourite brandy. It was the only way to preserve his body for the long journey home. My Lord would have enjoyed the joke.

I was left lying in the pale lantern light as Mr Beatty continued his grim work amongst the injured who seemed endless in number.

In my mind's eye it was a bright summer's day and the sun

glinted on the sea. I hovered between life and death and the desire to close my eyes forever was strong.

But then I heard the voice I most longed for in the whole world – a voice that would keep me tethered to this world. Harry was calling my name.

He scooped me up in his arms as if I weighed no more than a puppy, his voice rough from smoke and tears.

"I thought I had lost you, little maid," he said. "I thank God I have not."

I opened my eyes but barely recognised his sooty face; only the blue of his eyes was undimmed.

And then I remembered no more.

I slept for many hours and when I awoke at last it was to a world that had changed forever.

The French and Spanish fleets had been utterly destroyed; no longer could Bonaparte seek to send his troops onto English or Cornish soil. And yet what a price we had paid.

There was no feeling of being part of a great victory on board only the aching loss of our friend and leader, Lord Nelson: triumph seemed meaningless compared to what was lost for good.

Men went about their tasks as if stunned, faces blank with shock and disbelief. There was much work to be done: the remaining French and Spanish ships had to be secured and added to the British fleet before the coming storm broke; the Victory had to be repaired and made seaworthy as best as could be done. The shredded rigging was hacked away with axes and replaced with fresh rope. The decks were scrubbed clean of ash and blood and the sails patched and mended. Sailors had to be fed and life, such as it was, had to continue.

The cook, Mr Carroll, wept silently for the loss of his son as he went about his work feeding the hungry survivors as the storm clouds gathered.

After some discussion, I was allowed to rest on Nelson's own feather bed. He had no need for it and his love for me at his end was much spoken of. To those who had survived the hell of battle it was the only way they could show their enduring love of a gallant and brave man. It was his gentle kindness that I remembered best.

As I lay in a waking dream I felt the wounded ship rise and fall with the growing swell, the wind now moaning through the torn rigging.

The usual naval procedure would have been to drop the anchors and, indeed, this had been Nelson's order to Captain Hardy, so we could ride out the storm; but Victory's anchors had been shot away and there was nothing to be done but to run before the fury of the gale.

Harry came to check on me once and make sure I was as comfortable as possible. He stroked my head and placed a small piece of salted pork under the pillow, should I feel hungry at any time.

"I dursn't leave you a bowl of water, little maid," he said. "'Twould be scoaded about on the floor in no time. I'll come again when I can, but for now 'tis all hands to the pump."

He staggered back through the door of Nelson's cabin as another huge wave crashed into us. I closed my eyes, full of pity for the poor wounded men being tossed about in the belly of the ship. It was Nelson's wish that I be cared for and not a man on board would gainsay him, although I do not think that this care of me was begrudged in any way. 'Twas not the way of men on Nelson's ship.

The storm raged and roared above my head as the Victory was

swept through the towering seas for day after wearisome day.

Despite the violence of the weather I was strengthening with every hour that passed. I awoke to find that Harry had filled Lord Nelson's leather bucket with drinking water and hung it from a low hook.

If I timed the swing correctly I could take a mouthful of water before the bucket swung back to knock me from my paws.

It took several tries before I caught the knack and managed to drink my fill. I was so thirsty that I barely noticed that the water had an unpleasant brownish colour and tasted brackish. Every creature on board had to drink from the same fouled supply. That was expected on a long voyage – and I was too tired and thirsty to care. Besides, I was used to drinking from puddles that Harry would have turned up his nose at, even if full of a raging thirst.

I retrieved the salted pork from beneath my pillow and chewed slowly, surprised at how much energy it took to do that simple, natural act.

My wound was healing nicely, the new skin pink and shiny, the stitches itchy. Whether or not my fur would grow back, I knew not, but I would carry that scar until my dying day.

I lay in a meditative state, watching the moon cast fantastic shadows on the ceiling, listening to the rain rattling against the windows.

I was just falling into a deep and dreamless sleep when my ears pricked up: I heard the sound of distant voices calling out. I thought at first that it must be the crew on the Victory, but the sound was too tentative, too distant.

It was a sound I had heard two months ago, when lying beside Harry's fire in our little cottage: it was the sound of men afeared they were drowning.

I gave a sharp bark but there was no Harry nearby to hear me.

I tumbled off the bed, wincing from the pain in my side and limped out onto the deck. Harry and Walter were already there, their faces pale in the moonlight, their bodies obscured by the heavy oilskins that they wore to protect them from the fury of the night.

They were all gazing at something off the starboard bow.

"What is it?" called Captain Hardy, his voice raw from trying to be heard over the crashing of the waves.

"'Tis a lifeboat," cried Harry. "We're trying to get a line to her but..."

He shrugged helplessly. The chances of throwing a rope to a small rowing boat wracked by a surging storm were bleak. Nonetheless, the men tried. Over and over, using a leaded weight to try and throw the rope to the desperate men. But the wind buffeted the heavy rope as if it were a piece of cotton.

Once the little boat seemed to disappear entirely and I feared she had been crushed under the Victory's mighty prow, but she bobbed up again on the other side and Walter and Harry rushed to portside to resume their efforts.

An enormous wave hit the deck, rearing out of the night, a monster of the deep. We were all knocked from our feet, gasping, and then I saw Harry being dragged back into the sea.

The moment between thought and action was so brief that I can hardly be said to have thought at all. I grabbed the nearest rope I could find and leapt from the Victory.

Down I plunged, the icy water filling my eyes and nose and ears. I dared not cough because I would have had to let go of the rope which I was gripping with my teeth. It was the only thing attaching me to the Victory and my only hope of saving Harry.

I looked about me wildly, my keener night vision picking him out as the waves roared around me, buffeting me mercilessly. I kicked my legs, swimming as strongly as the cruel currents would allow.

Harry was a good swimmer but his heavy sou'wester and sea boots were dragging him down. I tried to reach him but every time I came close to him, the waves tore us apart again. I was beginning to tire. I was beginning to lose hope.

Suddenly the little lifeboat loomed up before me and I felt myself scooped from the water, bringing the rope from the Victory with me.

Voices shouted in the darkness.

But where was Harry?

I barked wildly.

I had saved the little boat but I had not saved Harry.

We lurched suddenly to one side and I saw a ghostly hand reach up to grab the gunwale. It was Harry! I barked again and this time the desperate men on the lifeboat turned and saw him and turned and helped. They pulled Harry into the boat where he lay gasping like a landed fish.

Neither had the Victory abandoned us.

Another line was got aboard and, one by one, all the exhausted men were hauled aboard, me tucked inside Harry's coat.

Harry and I were welcomed back on the Victory with a fierce hug from Walter Abbott that nearly flattened me.

"Strange time to go for a swim, Harry," said Walter, cuffing salty tears from his eyes.

"'Twas not swimming," said Harry, who was still coughing up seawater, "'twas time for a wash. I bathe once a year, whether I need it or not."

Harry found a scrap of material that turned out to be part of a French flag, and wrapped me in it, as I was shaking badly from the cold.

We then had leisure to look at the men we had saved from the small lifeboat. It was indeed a small group of Cape Trafalgar sailors, but they were not English, they were French. To my astonishment I saw that Dom Álvaro was among the wretched survivors.

It was a miserable, defeated enemy who stood before us and there was no pleasure in knowing that we had been the instrument of their downfall. They were just men. Sailors, like us, who had done their duty. And they had not prevailed.

Harry was peering at Dom Álvaro.

"I know you!" he said, in surprise. "You're that Portugee! You've been following me since Truro! You had me arrested back in Portsmouth."

"Yes," said Dom Álvaro. "I was tasked with retrieving certain documents from you. I regret that the instrument of your arrest was Major Dollard. He was not a gentleman, I fear."

He shrugged his shoulders and looked down at me. "It is of no matter. I failed in my task."

Harry shook his head slowly.

"No-one could have tried harder than you, sir. 'Tis no shame of yours," and he stepped forward to offer the enemy his hand.

Dom Álvaro looked up, straightened his back and grasped the hand of his erstwhile adversary.

"You have been a worthy opponent, Harry Carter. I salute you. It is strange, is it not, that we should meet again like this. You – and your dog – save our lives; we save yours and yet our beliefs divide us."

I do not understand humans. How can two good men be

mortal enemies? How can their ideas about the world be so different that they are prepared to lose their lives because of it, and yet honour each other, too?

And yet, and yet... seeing the expression on Harry's face, at times such as these, I can but suppose he thinks as I do. The world is a very strange place.

Dom Álvaro and his men were taken below, given food and dry clothes, and locked into the hold. Their fate would be to spend the rest of the war in an English prison. I did not envy them. I knew only too well what a miserable existence that would be. Such is war, even if you survive the battle.

⟫•⟪

The storm raged for a full week until, at last, we arrived, battered and bruised, into the harbour at Gibraltar.

It was only due to the great skill of the British sailors that not a single ship was lost. But many of the prize ships, so dearly won from the French, did not survive the journey. Just four out of 19 captured ships, limped to safety, crowded with the injured and a pack of surly prisoners of war.

The Gibraltar sun felt warm on my back as I stood, weak-legged on the quay. Harry staggered slightly, unable to keep his balance on the firm ground after two months at sea.

The news of our great victory and terrible loss spread swiftly. Many strangers came to shake Harry's hand because they had seen tears on his cheek, and conjectured, that he was an Englishman; and several, as they held his hand, burst, themselves into tears. Sorrow and consternation lay on every countenance but I, who grieved painfully, had no tears.

And among such sorrow, who notices the grief of a little dog?

Except, perhaps, the human she loves most in the world.

I was still weak from my wound so Harry picked me up and tucked me inside his jacket, just like when I was a puppy.

It was here that we parted company with Walter Abbott. He was for London, accompanying the great Admiral Nelson on his final voyage. But our work was done and we longed for home.

"God speed to you, Walter," said Harry. "If you are ever in Cornwall or in need of a friend, you know where to come."

They shook hands in silence, Walter stroked me gently, and then we parted.

CHAPTER TEN

A sad voyage home

Mourn for the brave
The immortal Nelson's gone
His last Sea fight is fought
His work of Glory done.

Placard at St Maddern's Church, Cornwall
Service of Thanksgiving, 1805

Harry and I were looking for a ship back to Cornwall. We were in luck. HMS Pickle was a fast little schooner that had been kept well back during the battle. Indeed, one broadside would have quite sunk her, but her crew showed their mettle by rescuing many survivors, of all nations.

As one of the fastest ships in the fleet, she was chosen to carry the news back to England. And the fastest route for any ship was to head for Cornwall and from thence the messenger would take a coach to London.

The captain was a man called John with the suspiciously French surname of Lapenotière. I sniffed his trouser leg cautiously but he smelled English. I decided to keep a weather eye on him all the same.

The crew were proud to carry anyone who had been on board the Victory with Nelson but, crammed as they were, with the injured and prisoners, it was a trifle more cosy than I would have liked.

Admiral Collingwood, now in charge of the fleet, had written the dispatch to tell London of the news, great and terrible as it was. It was given to Captain Lapenotière to deliver to the King with all haste.

As the dispatch was carried onto the Pickle, bound about with a black ribbon, Harry and I slipped aboard with far less ceremony.

The crew were eager to hear our first hand description of the battle and Nelson's death but Harry had not the heart to relive it, disappointing our new companions.

"Well," said a swarthy fellow by the name of Sam who had joined the crew from the Royal Sovereign, "that's a rum do and no mistake – although I hear that brandy is more his Lordship's tipple these days – fair soaked in it, I believe!"

He laughed uproariously at his own joke but Harry's lips grew taut at the ill-conceived humour. I raised my lip in agreement.

"Yes," continued Sam, "I never set eyes on Nelson, for which I am both sorry and glad, for to be sure I should like to have seen him, but then, all the men in our ship who have seen him are such soft toads, they have done nothing but blast their eyes and cry ever since he was killed. God bless you! Chaps that fought like the devil sit down and cry like a wench!"

Which, crudely as it was expressed, rather caught the mood on board, and it was a sombre crew that sat down to supper that night. The fact that we were outnumbered three to one by prisoners did little to improve the mood.

"You'll not believe this," said one Jack Tar with a musical Welsh lilt to his voice. "I was on guard duty for that lot o' Frenchies and Spaniards and you'll never believe it what happened."

"I dare say we won't, Merrick," said a wise old hand, "but why not tell us so we can decide for ourselves whether you be believable or not."

That was invitation enough for Merrick.

"Well," he said grandly, "I was on duty with all them enemy squashed into steerage with not enough chains to keep 'em quiet, and me as nervous as a long-tailed cat in a room full of rocking chairs when I hears 'em whispering, all secretive like and I knew then, sure as eggs is eggs that they was up to something. And..." he said, puffing out his chest, "I was right."

"What did you do?" said one of the cook's boys, his eyes wide as gobstoppers.

"I decided to stop 'em, boyo, that's what I decided."

"Fought 'em single-handed did you, Taff?" said one of the marines who was sitting at our table.

"And you don't speak Frenchie, Taff," said one sailor, "so how'd you know they was up to summat?"

Merrick ignored the interruptions and continued with his story. I got the impression that his regular crew mates were used to his highly colourful and elaborate way of telling a story.

"So I pretended I was a bit simple, see..."

"Not arf!"

"So I pretended I was a bit simple to put them at their ease but I made sure my musket was primed and ready. Then I says out loud that I only had another hour before the guard changed which was a good thing as I was feeling so sleepy. And they took the bait! But it wasn't another hour – it was the end of the last dog watch!"

There was a murmur of approval amongst the sailors and we all understood the import of what he'd said. I was surprised to find that the bristly little Welshman was cleverer than he looked, which when all is said and done, wasn't hard. But I shall explain for those not blessed with a nautical education.

The day at sea is divided into a series of 'watches' or duties. As no sailor could afford a timepiece (and salt water does somewhat interfere with the good working of a pocket watch), the duties are indicated by the ringing of a bell. That way no man, or dog, has the excuse of sleeping on and being late for a duty; you just have to listen out to the bells.

Merrick's watch finished at midnight but he made the Frenchies think he had another hour.

He continued with his story.

"So then Paddy over there surprises 'em by coming on duty just as they were about to rush me, and then there's two of us with primed muskets and suddenly they don't like the odds so much. So I says to Paddy, 'Look you, Paddy! Them Frenchies are hoping to slaughter us all in our beds tonight. Where are the Marines when you need them?' So he calls out the Sergeant and the marines are turned out right sharpish and you should have heard the grumbling! But I reckon as my quick thinking saved us all from being murthered in our beds!"

I had to admire the way Merrick turned a short story into an epic.

"Well, I was born under a lucky star, see," said Merrick proudly. "You'll be all right when you sail with me, boyos!"

I hoped he was right but we weren't home yet.

The storm that had had flayed the Trafalgar survivors caught us just off the coast of Brittany. The wind roared, tearing at the sails and we pitched about like a cork in a barrel and we were in danger of being driven onto the needle sharp rocks of Cape Finisterre, a twin of our Land's End, and a graveyard for incautious shipping.

Captain Lapenotière struggled onto deck in his heavy oilskins, his face white with tiredness and tension. Hundreds of souls were entrusted to him as well as Admiral Collingwood's Trafalgar dispatch – and he had to make the right decision. Some of the crew thought we should jettison the prisoners, but Captain Lapenotière was a humane man.

"We're carrying too much tonnage!" he shouted. "We're riding too low in the water – we shall sink if we carry on like this. I need a team of men to put four of our carronades over the side – it will lighten our load."

Harry and five other men attached ropes to the small cannon and used all their strength to move them. Heavy and awkward on a calm day, it was dangerous work in a storm; one slip and a man could be crushed to pieces by an unfettered gun carriage.

I stood in the pouring rain, my heart in my mouth, as the men struggled and heaved and finally managed to force four of the carronades over the side. I could see at once that the Pickle rode higher in the water and we were all happier for it.

The storm blew us off course and instead of being able to head north for England, we were blown full west.

After nine days of slogging through the storm, the winds quieted and we saw blue sky for the first time in weeks.

It was late at night and Harry was snoring in his bunk but I felt restless and had jumped down to take a stroll in the clear night air, but what I saw sent me scampering back to Harry.

Usually I am a thoughtful beast and would no more think of barking and waking sleeping men than of stealing their food, but today my heart was too full to be quiet. I barked loudly.

Several of the sailors cursed softly and a bleary-eyed Harry blinked down at me.

"What is it, little maid?" he said, rather crossly.

Well, I am clever at many things, but I have not yet learned to write messages or draw pictures, so all I could do was to bark again and urge him with a friendly nip at his breeches.

"All right, all right!" he said, rather grumpily. "I'm coming – you don't have to shout."

I begged to differ but at least he was moving.

Harry stumbled onto deck, rubbing his eyes.

I barked again to show my happiness and was rewarded by seeing a slow smile steal across Harry's face.

"Well done, little maid," he said. "Land ho!"

During the afternoon, the Pickle had flogged eastward away from the gales that had delayed our journey. We had passed English land in the night and now were drifting through the calm waters of Mount's Bay – and the Cornish coast was in sight at last.

Before our eyes lay the lights of the fairytale castle of St Michael's Mount. Could we but land, we were just a handful of miles from home.

Unfortunately the Pickle was bound for Falmouth and the captain would not waste time by putting into Penzance for our convenience. We would have to put up with the frustration of sailing right past our very cottage and ending up 20 miles further east.

Captain Lapenotière had joined us on deck, as delighted as we to see land at last. He ordered his Signal Lieutenant to run up a message that all ships might read: I Have Urgent Dispatches.

Any ship seeing that sign would make way for us and hope to hear the news as we passed. Every sailor in the land knew that the great Nelson had hoped to tame the Wolf of France in his own den.

Just then I espied a small lugger with red sails moving slowly westwards. They would pass right in front of us.

"Sir!" said Harry urgently. "My home is just beyond. Can we

– me and my dog – can we board yonder lugger and make for shore?"

We needed permission from the captain to leave the ship – I fervently hoped that he would give it to us.

He gave us a long stare.

"Very well," he said. "I would not deny a Victory man the chance to be with his loved ones. God speed to you, Mr Carter."

Harry held out his hand and Captain Lapenotière shook it warmly. Then Harry turned to the lugger.

"Ahoy there!" he roared. "Can you take us aboard?"

"Gorthugher da!" came back the greeting.

My heart swelled to hear the Cornish words, so long absent from my ears.

"Good evening to you! What news?"

"Napoleon is finished!" roared back Harry. "His fleet is finished!"

A ragged cheer went up from the Cornish fishermen.

I looked at Harry. He was saving the grimmer news for another moment. Let them cheer whilst they may.

Harry tucked me into his jacket and clambered down the netting that hung from the portside of the boat. The little lugger manoeuvred carefully towards us and at the opportune moment, Harry leapt from the Pickle, landing inelegantly in a pile of newly caught pilchards.

The fishermen thought this was great fun and were of a humour to leave us lying among their catch, making jokes about us being salted and sold at market along with the clouds of silvery fish.

Harry slithered to his feet, wiping fish scales from his jacket.

"I have news indeed," he said grimly.

The smiles of the honest fishermen died from their faces as

Harry related his news.

"That's put me all on a nupshot!" said the Master of the boat. "I had thought for another day's catch before putting into Newlyn, but we must hasten to Penzance for not a moment is to be wasted."

I was in full agreement. I longed for home with such a passion that I couldn't bear to be on this boat for another second.

The Master put the lugger about and set a fast sail for Penzance.

Within half an hour we were close to Cornish soil at last.

At last.

The fishermen grounded the lugger on the shingle and we leapt ashore.

"Mayor Giddy mun be told!" said the Master.

Harry agreed. This was the quickest way to spread the word and had the benefit of advising the gentry at the same time, saving us the tedious job of carrying the news from village to village.

"I'll go to the Mayor's house," declared Harry.

"No, wait!" said one of the fishermen. "He's up at that fancy dance in the Assembly Rooms – he'll be at his supper as we speak."

It was a short run from the water's edge up Chapel Street to the Assembly Rooms. I led the charge, turning to look over my shoulder at every fourth step, urging on the slow humans who followed me. Harry was last of all, his unsteady sea-legs making heavy weather of running on dry land.

Mayor Giddy was guest of honour at a ball. This puzzled me. I didn't know how anyone could be honoured by a ball. To me, a ball is something to be played with and chased when thrown. I soon learned that it meant something else entirely to humans;

it is a chance to eat too much food, drink too much drink and occasionally thunder about to music – although I believe they call it dancing.

We clattered into the Assembly Rooms, ignoring the protests of the doorman who, taking one look at our rough clothing, had determined to stop us.

"Let us through!" bellowed the Master. "We bring tidings of the war in France!"

Confusion, wonder and consternation interrupted the polished proceedings. Every head was turned towards us in astonishment. The Master went red in the face and started to mumble under his breath.

Harry nudged him in the ribs and encouraged him to point out Mayor Giddy. But I spotted him at once – a rotund man, who was girded about with a large brass chain. He looked too well fed to work for a living so I supposed him to be the one with whom Harry should speak.

I trotted over and Harry followed me as quickly as his trembling legs would allow.

"Sir!" said Harry. "I would fain speak a word with you – in private, sir. 'Tis most urgent."

The Mayor took one look at Harry's serious face and led him to a private audience in a smart room to one side of the main hall.

"Well, my man. What is it?"

"I come from France, sir. The French and Spanish fleets are defeated, sir, at Cape Trafalgar. We are safe from invasion."

The Mayor stared in astonishment. Whatever he had expected to hear, this was not it.

"This is tremendous news!" said the Mayor. "But on what authority do you know it?"

"We were with Lord Nelson on the Victory, sir. After the battle we made harbour at Gibraltar and from thence we boarded the Pickle with Captain Lapenotière. As we crossed the Bay, I fell in with these good fisherfolk who took us to shore. Even now the Pickle is making for Falmouth and the news will soon be abroad."

The Mayor's chest puffed out with pride.

"But we of Penzance knew of this first! 'Tis a fine moment for our town. We must go to the church to thank God for our deliverance."

He made as if to leave the room when Harry laid a restraining hand on the Mayor's velvet coat.

"There's more, sir. The battle is won but... Lord Nelson is lost. He was shot through and died aboard the Victory. They are taking his body for burial in London."

The Mayor's ruddy face turned grey.

"Truly? Lord Nelson is dead?"

He shook his head in disbelief and sorrow.

"'Tis true, sir. 'Tis sadly true."

The Mayor swallowed several times, gathering his thoughts.

"I must tell all of this sad news," he muttered. "I must... Thank you for bringing the news, terrible as it is. Please – eat and drink and rest. You must be quite fashed about after such travails."

But we had one more duty to perform.

Harry and the Mayor climbed up the wooden steps that led into the minstrel's gallery. From there they could look down in the ballroom.

A low whisper of conversation floated up to meet us but as soon as we were perceived, an expectant silence fell.

"Friends – I have important news to tell you. Great news and sad tidings. This gentleman has come from Lord Nelson's ship the Victory. He has travelled long and hard. The French and Spanish fleets were defeated off the coast of Spain at a place called Cape Trafalgar on the 21st this month past. There are, at this very moment, 19 prize ships on their way to Portsmouth

and hundreds of prisoners destined for our English gaols. But..." he held up his hands as a shout of joy filled the room.... "But that is not all. I have the sad duty to tell you that our great leader, Vice-Admiral Horatio Lord Nelson has been slain. He is gone."

There was a shocked gasp and intake of breath.

"I am now going to the church at Madron to thank God for our deliverance and to pray for the soul of a great man."

The people of Penzance that had so lately been celebrating now wended their way in procession. There was heartfelt rejoicing strangely mixed with mourning.

And the moment passed into memory.

Harry and I had mourned enough. We turned our faces eastwards and to home and walked towards the coming dawn.

THE END

Lord Nelson is laid to rest

At 9.45am on 4th November, the Pickle arrived in Falmouth. By noon, Captain Lapenotière was on his way to London in a hired post-chaise coach. The coach flew a Union Flag and a tattered French Tricolour. The week-long journey was completed in just 37 hours, the horses being changed no less than 19 times.

Captain Lapenotière reached the Admiralty at 1am on 6th November. He was greeted by the First Secretary of the Admiralty, Mr Marsden. The First Lord of the Admiralty, Lord Barham, was immediately woken to hear the tremendous news. The Prime Minister, William Pitt was informed at 3am and King George III and Queen Charlotte heard at 7am.

Guns were fired from the Tower of London, informing the general public that there was great news afoot.

Captain Lapenotière was presented with a silver pepper pot by the King, it being the first item His Majesty had to hand. He was also promoted to Commander. The Committee of the Patriotic Society gave him a sword worth 100 guineas.

Huge crowds attended five days of ceremonies and, finally, on 8th January 1806, Nelson's body was buried in the crypt of St Paul's Cathedral. The state funeral was on a scale never before afforded to a man born of humble birth. It was a demonstration of the widespread affection in which the dead hero was held.

Emma Hamilton was inconsolable and died in poverty.

End Note

During my research into the events described in this book, I came across a rare and important document housed in the cavernous vaults of the British Museum in London.

The document had lain, long neglected, amongst a pile of similarly dusty papers on the bottom shelf of a small display case assigned to the Documentation and Science Department. On closer inspection, I found that the fragile parchment with its faded, spidery writing was written in archaic Spanish. It turned out to be plans for the invasion of Britain via Cornwall, and the very manuscript that had set Pip on her adventures.

If you look closely, it is still possible to see the faint indentations caused by the teeth of a small black and white dog, although the scent of garlic sausage has long since faded.

J. A. C. West
August 2010

Bibliography

Madron's Immortal Legend: How the news of Trafalgar first came to England's shores *by Michael Dundrow*

Nelson: Britannia's God of War *by Andrew Lambert*

More Stories from J.A.C. West

PIP OF PENGERSICK – A SMUGGLER'S TALE

Adopted into a family of notorious Cornish smugglers, Pip of Pengersick takes to life on the high seas as she learns the trade of those who sail by a dark moon.

Business is going well when a well-dressed stranger sends Pip and her friend, the smuggler Harry Carter, on an urgent mission to London – ordered by the King of England himself.

A secret mission takes the intrepid Pip and Harry to France, a country in the grip of revolution. Pip's Cornish home seems a long way away – will Pip and Harry ever make it back alive without the shadowy figures who seem to dog their every footstep…

Winner of the Holyer An Gof Best Children's Book

LA BANDIDA – PIP GOES TO MEXICO

Pip's adventures take her to the land of Aztec treasure at the end of the eighteenth century.

How can Pip unlock the magic of the mysterious and deadly crystal skull? How can a Cornish maid survive in the hostile and mountainous land? Fighting off cougars, coyotes and bandits, Pip makes her way across Mexico searching for the lost treasure of an ancient civilization.

(Not yet published)

Tartu and the Pharaoh's Curse

Working on an archaeological dig in Egypt with her Uncle Howard, Tartu stumbles across the secret burial chamber of an ancient Pharaoh, uncovering a glittering treasure horde – and a deadly secret.

On her journey from the pyramids of Cairo to the catacombs of Alexandria, Tartu meets a kaleidoscope of memorable characters including the shambling camel Ata Allah; Dolly the donkey; Rhakotisa, the mad parrot of Alexandria; Alfred the army chimp (who is a bit too fond of home-made dynamite); and Tartu's dear friend and staunch companion, the elderly daredevil bulldog, Colonel Corpus Crunch.

Tartu races against time to solve the riddle of the sands and save the people she loves from an ancient evil and terrible foe.

Tartu's Close Encounter

What really happened at Windsor Castle the night the Queen's favourite corgi was abducted? Who are the mysterious visitors and what do they want?

Tartu's investigation of these strange events uncovers a plot of otherworldly dimensions. Accompanied by a motley crew of overfed, overweight and pampered corgis, Pericles the bad-tempered parrot and Toby, the royal gamekeeper's dog, Tartu's quest takes her on a difficult and dangerous journey across the English countryside to a place of ancient power.

Her search unwittingly reveals a secret that has been hidden for thousands of years – and an old enemy returns to haunt her.

Although a complete story in its own right, Tartu's Close Encounter follows on from the events described in Tartu and the Pharaoh's Curse.